Also by Jeramy Gates

He said, She said Detective Series

He said, She said "Murder"

Murder on the Lost Coast, A He Said, She Said Cozy Mystery

A Deadly Vintage

Ghost Story: A He Said, She Said Cozy Mystery

Valkyrie Smith Mystery Series

Should Be Dead

The Devil's Road

Dead End

Standalone

Erased

Watch for more at www.jeramygates.com.

Table of Contents

He said, She said #4

Ghost Story

By

Jeramy Gates

Published by Timber Hill Press

Chapter 1

TANJA SHEPHERD

I turned onto East River Road at ten p.m. on Friday. *Just a few more miles,* I thought. It had been a long day. I was exhausted, and I just wanted to be home.

Sturdy oaks lined the narrow, two-lane road. Gnarled branches shivered in the wind, falling leaves flashing in the headlight beams and slapping the windshield before vanishing into darkness. A dense fog hovered overhead, just brushing the treetops, the diffuse light of the full October moon casting an eerie glow across the mist-shrouded heavens. It was a little spooky, but I was relieved to be back in familiar territory.

My day had begun with a long drive up to Fort Bragg. It was a job for an insurance company –not the type of work Joe and I like to do, but they were willing to pay a hefty sum for our services. The task was simple: Photograph the charred remains of a burned-out house on the coast and verify that there weren't any other structures or losses of property. It would just take a few hours, and the fee would cover half of our monthly mortgage payment. We couldn't refuse.

Joe and I decided that I would make the drive alone. This left my husband at home with our daughter Autumn to save on daycare fees. It had seemed like a good idea at the time: A few hours of quiet time for me, some bonding time for Joe and our toddler. It was a win-win, or so I had thought. That was before I'd spent three hours driving up that winding, dangerous highway to Fort Bragg only to realize the lane I was looking for had been blocked by a fallen tree. The ensuing hike had taken nearly two hours, and the ice-cold coastal wind left me shivering uncontrollably by the time I got back to the Suburban. With chattering teeth, I headed into town looking for a bite to eat and a place to warm up.

I stopped at the *Sea Ranch Diner* for lunch. It was a cozy little restaurant on a cliff side lot overlooking the ocean. I warmed up with a steaming chowder bowl that may or may not have been the best I've ever had -if not, it was close- and from the comfort of my booth, gazed through the windows at the breakers crashing on the beach below. I watched the gulls materialize out of the mist only to vanish into the foamy water. I daydreamed about what it might be like to live in a place like that. It was so remote, so isolated, encompassed by the sheer beauty and power of the Mendocino coastline and the roaring Pacific. *It takes a certain type of person to live like that,* I thought. The type of person who might live alone on a mountain in Alaska, or singlehandedly circumnavigate the globe on a sailboat. *Joe should've come... He would love this.*

But Joe hadn't come. I had, and now I was paying the price for that decision. It had been a miserable trip, a terrible hike, and I still had hours to drive before I'd be back home. I stifled a tinge of jealousy at the thought of my husband playing by the fireplace with our daughter. I wasn't truly *jealous*. It wasn't that I wanted to switch places with Joe -I just wanted to be there, with him and Autumn, the way it should be on a foggy autumn day.

I lingered at the restaurant longer than I should have. As luck would have it, when I finally paid my bill and hit the road, I found out there had been an accident just outside of town. Traffic on the narrow stretch of Highway 1 leading south was at a standstill, and there was no way around.

The accident cost me a few more hours. Even after it was cleared, traffic was heavy because it had been backed up so long. There were dozens of us driving down that winding road, bordered on one side by steep mountains and the other by precipitous cliffs hanging out over the Pacific Ocean. Then the wind picked up, and it got dark...

And that's the story of how I ended up driving down those isolated, spooky roads alone late at night. I was bleary-eyed with exhaustion, and I just wanted to be home. I didn't even want dinner. I wanted to tuck Autumn in with a big hug, and then crawl into bed with Joe and cuddle. I knew I'd be asleep in minutes.

Halfway up East River Road, the trees opened up and the fog parted. I got my first good look at the sky since heading for the coast. It was clear and dark, filled with bright twinkling stars, and glowing with the silvery light of the full moon. My heart lifted a little. I was just minutes from home.

I came around a wide turn and saw headlights coming the other direction. I checked my speed and slowed a little. As the oncoming vehicle drew closer, I noticed a dark figure at the edge of the road. At first, it looked like an old signpost or the stump of a dead tree. I couldn't make out much more in the darkness. Then the figure began to move, and my eyes widened.

This was a person, I realized. It was someone dressed in dark clothing, starting to cross the road...

I tapped the brakes, bringing my speed way down. My headlight beams touched the figure, and I saw that it was an elderly man. He moved slowly, leaning heavily on a cane as he made his way across the pavement. I glanced at the oncoming vehicle. The driver wasn't slowing. Worried that he might not see the pedestrian, I flashed my high-beams. When that didn't make a difference, I tapped the horn.

The driver of the oncoming vehicle didn't seem to have a clue what was happening. A sense of impending doom came over me. My chest tightened, and time seemed to slow as the horrific events unfolded before me. *Move,* I thought, staring at the old man. *Hurry up!*

The next moment was the longest in my life. The high beams flashed through my vision, momentarily blinding me as the vehicle roared by. The driver slammed on his brakes, and the scream of tires split the night. I heard a sickening and unmistakable *thud* as the vehicle struck the victim.

I felt nauseous. I didn't want it to be real. I tried to tell myself that somehow the old man must have moved, or the truck might have missed him. Deep down I knew I was wrong.

At some point, I had come to a stop in the middle of the road. I glanced in the rear-view mirror, blinking spots of light from my eyes as the old blue truck came to a stop. I took a second to process everything. I was in danger, I realized, sitting in the road like that. I had no room to pull off, so I hurried around the corner up ahead, looking for a place to turn around. I saw the lights of a house down the road, overlooking the vineyards. There was a pullout there.

A few seconds after leaving the scene, I came racing back. To my shock, the truck was gone. I stared in disbelief as I slowed to a crawl and scanned the shoulder of the road, looking for the victim. I couldn't see the old man's body anywhere. There was no indication that what I had just witnessed had ever happened.

I looked around, confused. I *knew* this was the right spot. I had just been here, seconds ago. I pulled off the road and climbed out of the Suburban, cell phone in hand. The wind hit me like a splash of cold water. My chest rose and fell with hyperventilation-like rapidity and tears filled my eyes. I had left my jacket in the car, and goose pimples rose on my arms. I was too in shock to notice.

I scanned the darkness down the embankment. I couldn't see a thing. I turned, checking the slope on the other side of the road. Nothing there. I looked south, down the lane in the direction the truck had been driving. Again, nothing. It was dark, but not *that* dark. If someone had been there, I would have seen.

I dialed 911.

"What is the nature of your emergency?" said a pleasant female voice.

"I need the Sequoia Sheriff's Department," I said. It seemed like I could hardly breathe. A few seconds later, I heard, "This is the Sheriff's Department, Linda speaking. How may I direct your call?"

"Linda, it's Tanja Shepherd. I'm on East River Road, just south of Vine Hill. I just witnessed a hit and run."

"Do you need an ambulance?"

"Yes, hurry!"

"Nate is on duty tonight. He'll be there in just a minute."

"Thanks."

I activated the light on my cell phone, but couldn't see more than a few feet down the slope. I fought the urge to climb down the embankment and start searching the vineyard. I couldn't leave the road, or Nate might miss me. I couldn't do anything but wait for help.

I stood in darkness at the edge of the pavement. That poor old man was down that embankment somewhere, maybe dying at that very moment, but I couldn't do anything. It was the most helpless feeling I've ever experienced.

Chapter 2

JOE SHEPHERD

A strong wind blew through the sleepy little town of Vine Hill, shaking the dry leaves from the branches and howling through the eaves. The fire in the fireplace had burned low, leaving the house cool but not uncomfortable. Down the hall, Autumn slept peacefully in her little pink princess bed while I sat up late, alone in bed, watching television.

I wasn't really watching. I was too distracted. I was worried sick about my wife, who should have been home hours ago. It was almost two a.m. I had received a text from Tanja at eight p.m. letting me know that she was leaving Fort Bragg. The wording led me to believe she had sent it earlier -probably hours earlier since the message said she had stopped for lunch and was now on her way. That meant it was after noon when she'd sent it. Cell service is notoriously spotty along the coast. In many places, you're lucky to get it all. Her phone probably grabbed a signal long enough to spit out the text and then dropped it again. That was why I hadn't heard from her. At least I hoped that was it, and nothing more.

I had the TV down low, and I could hear the wind whistling and the tree branches slapping against the fence in the backyard. I hadn't tried calling Tanja in a while, so I picked up the phone and dialed again. Before it even rang, I heard the Suburban pulling into the driveway.

I heaved a sigh of relief. Tanja was okay. Whatever had happened to make her so late, it couldn't have been too bad. I headed down the hall in my pajamas, thinking up a few teasing lines along the way, because that is the only appropriate response when someone you care about has left you hanging all night:

What happened, did you get lost? Did the GPS accidentally send you to Death Valley again? How many states away did you get before you decided you couldn't live without me?

Then the door opened, and my grin vanished. The woman standing before me was a shell of her former self. Eyes red from crying, face streaked with tears and running makeup, her long blonde hair a wild mess from standing in the wind. I barely recognized my wife.

"Are you all right? What happened?"

Tanja rushed into my arms. "Joe, it was horrible. I can't... I can't even describe... You won't believe me. No one else does."

These words poured out of her in a meaningless jumble. I couldn't make sense of it. Had there been an accident? That must be it. But I glanced over her shoulder and saw that the Suburban was fine. Not a dent or scratch. Maybe she had witnessed a horrible car crash. That would explain her being this upset.

I led my wife into the kitchen and started a pot of coffee. Tanja was shaking, not so much from the cold as from distress. I grabbed a blanket from the living room sofa and draped it over her shoulders. I fixed her a cup of San Francisco Blend with a teaspoon each of sugar and milk, just the way she likes it. I handed her the steaming mug and settled into the chair across from her.

"All right," I said, reaching out to touch her hand. "Tell me the whole story."

Tanja looked into my face, her gorgeous hazel eyes glistening. She went on to describe in vivid detail the accident she had witnessed, right down to the color of the truck. She told me how Nate had arrived and helped her search the area for the body. When the ambulance got there, the EMTs joined in the search, too. An hour of scouring the vineyard and crawling up and down the embankment had led to nothing. By the time it was over, they were convinced that she had been hallucinating.

"You had a long drive," Nate had said, trying to console her. "Exhaustion plays tricks with the mind. It can make you see things that aren't really there..."

But Tanja had insisted she *had* seen it, and she still insisted it, sitting there with a mug of coffee in her hands and a blanket wrapped around her like a lost little girl. She looked so distraught, so overwhelmed that I didn't know what to say.

"You need to get some sleep," I told her. "In the morning, we'll drive down there and take a look."

"Joe, I can't... I have to go back. He's still there, somewhere. He could be dying *right now!*"

Oh. I took a deep breath. "All right, I'll go take a look. You stay here with Autumn."

She seemed reluctant to agree. Tanja was ready to go right back out into the cold. She was that upset. "No," I said reading her thoughts. "We can't call someone to watch Autumn in the middle of the night, and we don't need to wake her up and drag her out in the cold. You wait here. Let me do this."

Tanja relented. I headed for the garage to find a good flashlight.

Fifteen minutes later, I was climbing down the embankment in the exact spot Tanja had described. The wind was howling, and it was ice cold. I had worn a nice warm coat and leather driving gloves, but it hadn't even occurred to me to bring a hat. Soon, my shaved head was tingling with cold and my ears were burning. My eyes watered so much I could hardly see.

I heard a suspicious noise in some bushes along the road. I went to investigate, and for my troubles, nearly got sprayed by a skunk. I backed away in a hurry, and the creature went skittering across the pavement and up the adjacent hill. A thorough inspection of the bushes revealed nothing else of interest.

I stomped through the edges of the vineyard, shining the beam of my flashlight into every possible nook and cranny. I found an irrigation ditch about thirty yards south of the scene. It was dry, and I saw no indication that anyone had been in the area. In fact, the vineyard soil was hard and dry everywhere. The rain hadn't started yet. If by some crazy chance the old man had managed to walk away from the scene, it would be impossible to track him.

Just to satisfy my own curiosity, I headed down to the river. It was a half-mile hike west of the road. When I arrived, I found the water level low enough that I could easily search the trees and brush along the banks. I found a long stick, and used it to poke and prod through the bushes.

An hour later, I had made enemies out of half a dozen more critters but still hadn't seen a sign of the missing old man. Defeated, I returned to the car shivering and exhausted. I wanted to believe the man was real -that my wife's story wasn't a sign of some delirium- but I couldn't find a single clue upon which to found any hope. By the time I left, I was more worried about my wife than the mysterious old-timer.

When I woke later that morning, the sun was shining in through the bedroom window. I glanced at the clock. It was ten-thirty. The weather outside was cool and breezy, and I saw the branch of a neighbor's oak tree laying on the ground in the backyard. Thankfully, it had missed the fence on its way down.

"Morning," Tanja said as I came down the hallway in my robe. She was at the computer desk. Autumn was on the floor, playing. I kissed my wife and then knelt down to give my daughter a hug. I spent a few minutes playing with her before making my way to the kitchen for a cup of coffee. When I came back into the living room, I realized that my wife had opened up Google Earth on the computer.

"What are you looking at?" I said.

"Just checking the area around the accident."

The accident. So she was still convinced it had happened. I fought back the temptation to tell her I'd spent half the night out there in the cold, and nearly suffered frostbite without finding so much as a footprint or a drop of blood.

"Find anything?" I said, trying to sound supportive.

"It's very strange," she said in an absent voice. "I know we crisscrossed that area several times last night. And he couldn't have gone far; there's nowhere to go."

"Uh-huh."

"I did some calculations. I think at most, the old man might have been thrown thirty feet from the crash scene. That includes the elevation of the embankment. He should have landed in the vineyard. But that can't be what happened, because we searched the whole area. Then I thought, maybe the truck didn't hit him as hard as I thought -maybe it just swiped him, and the man may have simply wandered off in a daze. He could have gone in any direction. There's a house just up the road-" She frowned. "Why are you looking at me like that?"

"Like what?" I said.

"You think I'm crazy, don't you?"

"Of course not. But you do have to admit, the whole thing is a bit strange. I walked all over that area last night. I even walked down to the river."

She stared at me, her beautiful eyes impossibly wide, long blonde bangs framing her high cheekbones. "And?" she said.

I sighed. "Nothing. Not a hint."

"We have to go to that house, Joe. He must have wandered back there. Maybe it's where he lives."

"You're not going to give up on this, are you?"

"Would you?"

"Fine. What about Autumn?"

"We'll bring her with us. We can swing by the park on the way home."

I resigned myself to the fact that it was going to be a long day. I headed back to the bedroom to get dressed.

Chapter 3

TANJA

I'm *not* crazy. Unfortunately, that's exactly what a crazy person would say. No wonder the people in those Alfred Hitchcock movies always lose their marbles. The first time you say or do something out of the ordinary, people start wondering. From there on, you're on the defensive. You have to prove you're *not* losing your mind, and the mere act of trying to prove it is enough to make you lose it. You can't prove a negative. Anyway, Joe believed me. Or, at least he was trying to.

The house I'd found was a small single-story ranch on the west side of the road, overlooking the vineyards. It was old, and the cracked and peeling brown paint looked like it hadn't been retouched in decades. The single oak tree out front took up most of the cramped yard, but the owners had still somehow managed to stuff a plastic prefab shed in there, and a rusty old swing set, too. To the right of the house, a dirt road led down to a big barn and a graded parking lot full of tractors and vineyard equipment.

"This is the place?" Joe said, slowing as we approached the property. I nodded. He pulled off the road and parked next to the house. "I wonder who lives here."

"We're about to find out," I said. "Stay here with Autumn. I'll be right back."

It was cool and windy. I pulled my jacket close and jammed my hands into the pockets as I approached the house. I caught a glimpse of someone peeking out through the living room curtains. The face vanished, and the front door opened as I arrived on the doorstep. An elderly Hispanic woman appeared. She was in her early eighties, frail and silver-haired with a shawl wrapped around her shoulders.

"Yes?" she said with a heavy Spanish accent. I introduced myself and apologized for bothering her. She said her name was Mary.

"I was just wondering if you witnessed an accident last night," I said. "It would have been late. Around midnight."

"Here?" she said, gesturing at the road in front of the house.

"Yes, just a little way down the road. I believe a truck hit someone."

Mary frowned at me. "No, I see nothing like that."

"You're sure? Was anyone else here?"

"No, we see nothing," she said.

"Maybe if I could just-" The door closed. Mary was done answering my questions.

As I stepped away, I glanced through the living room window. I couldn't see anything in the darkness behind the curtains. I wondered if someone else was in there, or if Mary was alone. Back in the car, I told Joe what had happened.

"She's probably an illegal," he said. "That would explain her caginess."

"I understand that, but I'm not a cop. Why would she be so nervous about answering a few questions?"

"Wouldn't you be? She doesn't know who you are. Besides, you found out what you wanted to know, right?"

"I did?"

"Sure. She didn't see anything. Neither did anybody else. I don't see why she would lie about that."

He was right. Mary might have been nervous about talking to me, but if she was guilty of anything, it was most likely her immigration status. If an injured man had come to her last night, I don't think Mary would have lied about that.

Joe and I didn't discuss it any further. We drove to the park, where I sat at a picnic table and watched as Joe crawled around the big wooden fort with our daughter. Autumn was in absolute heaven, running back and forth across the suspended bridge, swinging on the tires that dangled from chains below. The two of them played hide and seek, and Joe pretended not to be able to see her until Autumn jumped out and squealed. It was hilarious to watch them interact in that way. It was exactly what I needed to let go of the stress that had been eating at me.

While we were there, Grandma called to invite us up to the vineyard for dinner. I agreed. I didn't even consult Joe. No one *ever* turns down Grandma's barbecued ribs. But first, we had to feed Autumn lunch and give her a nap. Joe and I decided we needed one, too. It had been a rough night.

We drove back home, and not long after Autumn went to sleep, Joe and I did as well. In my dreams, I saw the accident replaying in mind like a looped video. I saw flashes of the old man in the headlights and heard the roar of the truck's engine and the scream of its tires as the brakes locked up. I saw the body stretched out on the ground, the man's vacant gaze staring up at me, his lips moving as if to speak, but I could hear no words. I called out for help, but no one came. When I looked back down, he was gone. A sense of gloom and anxiety came over me, and it seemed like I couldn't escape the darkness.

I woke feeling hungover and depressed. Joe pampered me, like he always does, fixing coffee and helping Autumn get ready to go to Grandma's. A short while later, we were on our way to Alexander Valley.

"Hello, dear," Annette said when she met us at the door. "Are you feeling better?"

I cringed. I had forgotten that Nate had been at the scene last night. Grandma and Sheriff Diekmann must have heard all about it by now. I bent over to give Annette a big hug (she's a slender five-four, and I stand right at six feet. I tend to tower over most women, Grandma in particular). I reassured her that I was fine, and then changed the subject: "What's that wonderful smell?"

"I've been slow-cooking the ribs all afternoon." She winked. "I know, it's cheating, but they're so much better that way. Bill can throw them on the grill as soon as we're ready."

We were in no hurry. Annette and "Grandpa Bill" took turns holding Autumn while we got caught up. The sheriff informed us that he had finalized his retirement plans, and by the end of the year, it would be official. The sheriff's retirement was phase one of the couple's strategy. Phase two was their marriage, which was still in the planning stages, and the third phase was their winery, which would occupy the couple's full attention in the coming years.

Her first year's production had made an impressive showing at auction that spring, and over the summer, Annette had hired a professional to help get her product to market. Since then, she'd sold out her entire inventory and had orders stacking up. The couple would need to hire a crew and renovate the barn for on-site commercial winemaking in order to keep up with demand.

"I have a second year's worth bottled and ready to go," Annette explained, "but it's in storage for now. I won't sell it until it's ready. A well-structured red needs at least a year in the barrel and two more in the bottle. Maybe even three."

"Two's a minimum," Diekmann added. "Unlike that mass-produced swill, we take pride in our product."

"Good for you," I said. "I'm glad to see it's working out. You both deserve it."

We headed out back to enjoy dinner on the redwood deck. It was a warm evening, with just a slight breeze shaking the vines and cooling the air. The sunset was a spectacle of brilliant reds, purples, and oranges spanning from horizon to horizon, and Autumn was in awe. So much so that it was a struggle to get her to eat.

After a little more small talk, the conversation inevitably took the turn I had been dreading: "So tell us about your ghost story," Annette said. "Nate made it sound so spine-tingling."

I groaned inwardly. *So now it's a ghost story?* I looked around the table and found them all staring back at me. Even Joe, although he wore a sympathetic expression and gave me an encouraging nod. What choice did I have? They didn't mean anything by it. They weren't trying to be insulting or patronizing. They were just curious.

I took a deep breath, organized my thoughts, and told them the whole account. By the time I was done, Grandma seemed to have been sufficiently spine-tingled, and Diekmann wore a dark look that made me wonder if I had said something to upset him. He didn't say anything though, and by the time dessert was on the table, all was forgotten. We dove into Grandma's peach cobbler like starving jackals, and digested it over a fresh pot of coffee.

Autumn was asleep in Joe's arms when we left. He was already halfway down the porch stairs when Diekmann said something that gave me pause. I stood on the front porch, my hair twisting in the breeze as Joe went rushing to the Suburban to get Autumn into her car seat.

"You know, there's something familiar about that story you told us," the sheriff said.

"Familiar? In what way?"

"It reminded me of an old cold case; something that happened in that area a few years back. I don't remember the details. It's probably just my imagination. Old age sometimes makes the mind fuzzy."

"I must be getting old, too," I said with a laugh.

We said goodnight, and I hurried to the car to get out of the cold. On the way home, I told Joe what Diekmann had said.

"Well, there you go," my husband said. "See, that makes sense."

"What do you mean?"

"How many times have we been through that old box of cold cases? Half a dozen, at least."

"But what does that have to do with what I saw last night?"

"I don't know... Maybe something about the drive triggered a memory-" He stopped short as he realized I was glaring at him. "Not that I don't *believe* you," he added hastily. "'Cause I know what you saw was real."

I crossed my arms, leaned back in the seat, and didn't say another word all night.

Chapter 4

JOE

Sunday morning dawned bright and sunny, and for a while, it seemed things were off to a good start. Tanja appeared to have forgotten her frustration with me. We had a nice breakfast of bacon and eggs, which Autumn turned into a slurry on her plate and threw halfway across the kitchen. I dutifully cleaned up while Tanja took our daughter for a bath.

I had just finished wiping down the wall adjacent to the high chair when the doorbell rang. It was Nate. "Diekmann wanted me to drop this off for you," the deputy said, handing me a plain manila folder. "Said you talked about it at dinner last night, I guess."

I recognized it as one of Diekmann's cold case files. "We talked about this?" I said. I had no idea what he was talking about. After my spat with Tanja, I'd put the entire thing out of my mind.

Nate shrugged. "He said you'd know. Anyway, you can drop it off when you're done with it."

I gave him a somewhat perplexed "Thanks." Nate headed for his cruiser. The instant I closed the door, it all came back to me. Diekmann *had* said something to Tanja about one of his files. He said the event my wife had witnessed resembled one of his old cases. But why the sheriff felt it important enough to send over the file, I couldn't imagine. A cold case couldn't possibly have anything to do with the accident Tanja had seen. Could it?

No, it didn't make sense. What would a years-old criminal investigation have to do with a hit and run two nights ago? I heard Tanja call from the down the hallway, "Who was that?"

"Just some mail," I said. I didn't want to rehash the argument we'd had the night before. I put the file in the kitchen, figuring I might bring it up later. Or maybe never.

Tanja brought Autumn out wrapped in a towel, and they plopped down on the sofa. Tanja proceeded to dry her off, and then started to brush Autumn's hair. Halfway through this process, my wife started in on me:

"So, who did you say was at the door?"

"Just mail," I mumbled over my shoulder. By then I was sitting at the computer, looking at cool cars that I'd never own. Classics, mostly. I have a thing for old hot rods: Deuce coups, Model Ts, stuff like that. I used to see them everywhere as a kid. Growing up just a few miles north of the place where George Lucas shot *American Graffiti,* hot rods were practically a religion around here. Unfortunately, those days are long gone. Now, it seems just millionaires can afford them, and nobody drives those cars for fear of damaging them.

"We got a package?" my wife persisted, pulling me away from my fantasy shopping trip.

I turned to look at her, frowning. "A package? Why would you say that?"

"Because it's Sunday, Joe, and the only mail that comes on Sunday would be a special delivery. Did you order something from Amazon?"

Crap. I searched my mind for a better explanation, but the guilt on my face must have been painfully obvious. That's the trouble with marrying a body language expert. She always knows when you're lying.

Tanja glared at me until I rose from the chair and hurried into the kitchen to retrieve the file. I came back with it in hand, like a corrected puppy with his tail between his legs. "Here," I said, handing it to her. "Don't say I didn't warn you."

I dropped into the desk chair and watched her open the file with one hand while she held Autumn with the other. After a few seconds, Tanja set Autumn down on the floor and began to flip through the rest of it.

"Joe, do you know what this is?"

"One of Diekmann's files."

"Obviously. Don't be a jerk."

"I knew this would happen."

Her eyes narrowed to slits. "You knew *what* would happen?"

"I knew if I gave you that file, you'd get like this again."

She started to say something, hesitated, and instead handed me a printout from inside the file. It was a color photocopy of a man's picture. He appeared Caucasian, but his tanned, weatherworn skin, dark eyes, and high cheekbones led me to believe there was some Native American blood there, too. I guessed his age to be around seventy.

The man wore a brown tweed suit, the kind my grandfather used to wear, and leaned on a hardwood cane. He had a bolo tie around his neck with some sort of red stone set into the center. Due to the way he gripped his jacket lapel, I noticed that he had a matching stone set into the ring on his left hand.

"Okay," I said, staring at the photo. "What do you want me to see?"

"That's *him,* Joe. That's the man I saw the other night."

I felt a chill crawl down my spine. I wasn't quite sure why, but I knew it wasn't good. "Huh?"

"His name is Charles Martingale. He's a missing person. According to this file, he disappeared ten years ago."

"Then it can't be him."

She dismissed me with a roll of her eyes. She went back to reading the file. I watched for a moment until I saw her jaw drop and her eyes widen. She covered her mouth with her hand. She scanned a bit farther down the page and then looked up at me, her face ashen and eyes wide. "Oh my God," Tanja whispered.

"What is it?" I said. "What's wrong?"

"Joe, this happened in the same spot where I saw it Friday night. *Exactly* the same spot. The single witness was another driver who remembered seeing an old blue truck on the road that night."

"It's just a coincidence. It can't be..."

Tanja rose to her feet, file still in hand. She started reading the file and pacing at the same time. "They found blood," she said without looking up, "but never found a body. The man's wife - Oh my God, it's Mary!"

"Mary?"

"The woman from the house. She's his wife, Joe. No wonder she didn't want to talk to me." She froze, the blood draining from her face. "Charles disappeared on the night of October 4th, ten years ago. It was the exact same *date!*"

I gave her a baffled look. "You're telling me the accident you witnessed last night-"

"Is exactly what happened ten years ago, to the day!"

"And you're sure it was the man in that photo?"

"I couldn't forget him, Joe. Not after what I saw. Look, he even had the same cane."

As dubious as it all sounded, I know that my wife is no liar. Plus, she's one of the smartest people I've ever met. So, if she said the man she'd seen was Charles Martingale, then maybe it was. I shrugged. "I guess maybe you really did see a ghost."

"But Joe, that's..." she gave me a look that I couldn't quite interpret. I thought I understood. She had *seen* this accident happen with her own eyes. She knew, in her mind, that it was real. Therefore, it couldn't have been a ghost, or a vision, or anything like that. But it was also impossible. So, how do you reconcile something like that?

"Look on the bright side," I said, trying to inject some optimism into the conversation. "You saw something terrible, but it wasn't *real.* It was a memory, like an apparition; something like that. I've heard about this stuff before. Remember that TV show, Ghostfacers?"

"But it *was* real, Joe. That's the problem. Don't you see? This man is a real person, and he's still missing. His wife has been living without him for ten years, and with no idea what became of him."

I considered that. "Unless she killed him," I said. "Maybe *she* was the one driving the truck."

"Oh, I suppose that's possible. Of course, there's just one way to find out."

"Here we go," I said with a groan.

"What? Do you honestly want to just walk away from this?"

"We're private investigators," I said. "We have a business. We get *paid* to find a missing person. We can't just spend our time chasing down ghosts. We'll go broke."

"Remember the pictures I took at the coast? That's half our mortgage payment."

"And what about the rest of it?"

"We can afford a couple of days, Joe."

I sighed. I knew I was beat. My wife was not going to let this go until we had exhausted every avenue. "We still have that agreement with Diekmann," I grumbled. "Maybe he'll pay us if we can close this case."

Tanja's face lit up, and she let out a cheer. "Great! I'll get my coat."

"What for? Where are we going?"

"To interview the witness."

"What witness?"

"The woman who saw the truck, remember?"

Groan. This mystery had a hold on her. The only time -and I mean *only* time- my wife gets carried away with herself is when she's in pursuit of a mystery. Everything else just sort of fades into the background.

"That was ten years ago-"

"I have all of her information right here," she interrupted. "She works in Sebastopol..."

"Don't you think you should call first?"

Tanja gave me a look. She reached for her cell phone, which was on the end table, and started dialing. She dialed the number, listened for a moment, and hung up. "Disconnected," she said.

"Oh well," I started to say, thinking I might have weaseled out of it. But immediately she began dialing again. I heard a muffled female voice at the other end of the line, and Tanja said:

"You're open? Great! Is Jan Flowers available? Oh, that's all right, I'll just swing by." She hung up, grinning from ear to ear. "She still has her business."

Ten minutes later, we were on our way to Sebastopol.

Chapter 5

TANJA

Sebastopol sits on Highway 116 about halfway between Santa Rosa and the Pacific Ocean. It's a quaint, somewhat sprawling little town, with an unusual combination of modern development, old farmhouses, subdivisions and rolling vineyards. The community is eclectic and artistic. Metal junk sculptures decorate front yards and road signs proclaim strange, vaguely political slogans that don't quite make sense, like: *"War is Murder - Save the Trees!"* or, *"Mannequins are People too!"* posted next to a mannequin painted army green and dressed in fatigues.

Anyone not from California will recognize this behavior as uniquely Californian, and possibly drug-induced. Locals hardly even notice. If California is the home of the strange and unusual, northern California is the center of that universe.

According to Diekmann's file, the one potential witness to the event was a woman named Jan Flowers. She owned a pottery shop just off South Main Street. Joe was driving. Autumn was in her car seat in the second row, happily sucking on a sippy-cup of apple juice. On the way there, I read aloud Jan's statement from the file.

"That's it?" Joe said when I had finished. "She saw an old blue farm truck?"

"Ford," I reminded him. "Details are important. And the description matches what I saw, too."

"Uh-huh. She didn't have many details ten years ago. She'll have even fewer now."

"Maybe," was all I said.

It wasn't hard to locate the pottery shop. It was situated on a large corner lot. The entire lot, even the parking area, contained examples of Jan's pottery scattered and stacked in reckless disarray. A ten-foot Buddha statue sat alone in a quiet corner, while bowls and platters were stacked ten feet high right in the middle of a nearby parking space.

"She keeps herself busy," Joe mumbled as we parked in one of the few empty spaces. At the far end of the lot, several people worked to load a fountain onto the bed of a truck. The base alone must have been six feet across and weighed several hundred pounds. Other customers were moving around the lot, browsing the inventory and shuffling in and out of the low, flat-roofed building in the corner.

It was noon, and the sun was beating down as we climbed out of the Suburban. The temperature had shot up into the low eighties, as it often does in Sequoia in October, but there was a nice breeze coming in from the coast. A gust tousled my hair and cooled my face as I tucked Autumn into her stroller.

I caught the scent of onion rings and cheeseburgers drifting from a burger joint down the street. I wasn't terribly hungry, but the smell was divine and it made my stomach rumble. It also reminded me that we hadn't brought anything to feed our toddler. Autumn's appetite is like a ticking time bomb. By the time she starts making noise, it's already too late.

As we began casually browsing the lot, I kept an eye on the group with the fountain. I was sure that Jan was the woman who seemed to be directing the group in the loading process. She had the thin, strong physique of an active, hard-working woman, and an air of confidence that implied this was her place. She wore her auburn hair pulled back in a ponytail, and her jeans and tank top had the stains and wear consistent with work in the pottery business. She was quite occupied for the moment, so Joe and I wandered into the building to look around.

If the disorder in the parking lot had seemed chaotic, the shop was frighteningly worse. Pottery sat stacked up to the ceiling in the corners and against the walls, and lay strewn haphazardly along the aisles. Rows of shelves bent under the weight of bowls, platters, vases and figurines. It was nearly impossible to move the stroller through the tiny, cramped space. When we encountered another customer, it was like two semi-trucks meeting on a one-lane road going opposite directions. After a few minutes of that, Joe took Autumn out of the stroller, folded it up, and handed it to me.

"Hello there," said a woman's voice. "Can I help you find anything?" We turned to see Jan standing in the doorway. We introduced ourselves as investigators working with the Sheriff's Department. Jan confirmed she was the person we were looking for, and Joe said, "We'd like to ask you about an accident you witnessed a few years ago."

She gave us a confused look. "What sort of accident?"

"It wasn't actually an accident," I chimed in. "The police report said you saw a vehicle in the vicinity of a disappearance. There was a suspected hit and run..."

"Oh, that. I haven't thought about that in years. What do you want to know?"

"We've read the police report, but we're hoping you might remember something you previously overlooked. Can you think of any details you might have missed?"

"Like what?"

"Did you get a glimpse of the driver?"

"I did, but it was very brief. I was coming home from a date that night -I lived in Vine Hill at the time- and I was tired and upset. The date hadn't gone well and I just wanted to be home. I remember being almost home when I saw that truck parked in the middle of the road. It seemed so strange, you know? Dangerous."

"It was parked?" I said.

"Yes. I slowed down, thinking there might have been an accident. I saw a man standing at the tailgate, fussing with something in the bed of his truck. I started to roll down the window to ask if there was anything wrong, but he looked up at me and gave me a glare that chilled me to the bone. It was hateful, you know? Like he wanted to kill me. I was so scared that I stomped on the gas and got out of there."

"And then you contacted the police?"

"No, I just tried to put it out of my mind. Several days later, I heard my friends talking about the old man who had gone missing that night. It seemed like a strange coincidence, so I called the police and told them what I had seen."

"Who questioned you?" I asked.

"I wasn't really questioned -not in so many words. I called the sheriff's office and told them what I had seen. They thanked me, and that was it."

"There was never a follow-up?" Joe said.

"No. Should there have been?"

Joe and I exchanged a look. "What about the man you saw?" I said. "Can you describe him?"

She stared off into the tree branches. "He had dark hair. Brown maybe, slightly curly. And dark eyes -I could never forget those eyes. I can't say how tall he was. He was hunched over at the back of the truck, fussing with something. The whole thing seemed eerie. That's why I called the police, but I guess they didn't think much of it."

"Can you remember any other details?" Joe said. "The report said it was a blue Ford truck?"

"Yes, like a ranch truck. It was very beat up. Lots of dents and rust."

"What about the year?"

"I wouldn't know. It was one of the older ones -the big boxy ones with round headlights. My uncle had one like that when I was in elementary school. You remember those?"

Joe said that he did. We thanked her and assured Jan that she had been very helpful.

I gave Joe a smug look as we pulled out of the parking lot. He rolled his eyes. "Okay, she may have remembered more than I expected. Still doesn't help us, though. All we know is that a dark-haired guy in a blue Ford truck was in the vicinity, acting strange. He might not even be connected with the disappearance. Either way, we'll never find him."

"I'm not giving up yet. She did describe the truck."

"Yeah, an old farm truck. Can't be many of those around. Ten thousand, twenty maybe."

"You're exaggerating."

"How will we find it?"

"We may not have a license plate number, but we do have a fairly accurate description."

"Not really. She said it was *boxy.* That could describe any truck from the sixties through the eighties. Again, we're talking thousands."

"So, we narrow it down. How many were registered in this county? How many in Vine Hill, and nearby towns? And remember, they have to be blue. And round headlights."

"It's a long shot."

"We have to start somewhere."

Joe sighed. "I suppose Diekmann might give us access to the DMV database in his office. If we were officially on the job, that is."

"What about the NCIC?"

"Criminal records? What good will that do?" Then understanding dawned on his face. "You're thinking the hit and run driver might have a record."

"Why not? We're looking at two possibilities here: Either it was an abduction, or a hit and run where the body was taken by the driver to avoid discovery. In either case, we're probably talking about someone with a history. If we can narrow down the list of owners and then cross-reference them with NCIC-"

"Then we'll have our most likely suspects," Joe finished. "It won't work, though. Forget it."

"Why?"

"Because you don't work with the FBI anymore, remember? They are very picky about who can use the National Crime Information Center. Permission is granted on a case-by-case basis, and it's not for civilians. Trust me, we're not getting access. Not even if Diekmann wanted to. If it was a specific individual, with probable cause or something like that, the sheriff could do it. But he would have to run the search and then share the information with us."

"All right. Public records, then. We can still search courthouse records, right?"

"Shouldn't be a problem."

"Good. At least we will know if the person has a record in Sequoia County."

"Good thinking," Joe said. "Sounds like you have this case under control. Maybe I should just go home and take a nap."

"Very funny. You're not going anywhere."

We picked up lunch at the aforementioned burger joint and took it to eat at a nearby park. It was a quick fix and not terribly expensive, but I still cringed at the idea of spending the money. Autumn took a few bites of fries and then ran for the playground clutching a chicken strip in one hand. I frantically called after her not to eat while playing or she would choke, and then winced as I realized how much I sounded like my mother. Joe saw the look on my face and shot me a wicked grin.

After eating, I made a call to sheriff Diekmann. He agreed to meet us back in town and said that if we could solve the case, he would pay us according to our previous agreement.

Now, it was official. It was time to get to work.

Autumn finished her lunch on the way back to Vine Hill, leaving me a nice mess to clean up in the Suburban. Before going in to meet Diekmann, we put our daughter in her stroller with a sippy-cup and a nice cozy blanket. She was asleep before we even made it to the front desk.

Sheriff Diekmann met us inside. "I'll log you in," he said, "but first I need to remind you: Your work as consultants is based on results. If you don't solve the case..."

He didn't need to finish. We'd had the same conversation several times. I assured him that we were fine with the terms, and that we were sorry for making him come in to work on a Sunday. "Doesn't bother me," he said. "I'm on call all day, every day. You'd better take advantage of it while you can, because in a few months, I'll be gone."

This was in reference to his upcoming retirement. Joe and I were both very happy for him, but I think at a certain level, we both worried about the implications for us, professionally. Diekmann's consultation checks had helped us out of more than one financial tough spot. In a way, we had come to count on that agreement as a safety net. With him gone, there was no telling if the new sheriff would uphold that agreement. By Christmas, our safety net might be gone.

Joe and I went to work. My DMV search was restricted to vehicles currently in the database; anything unregistered for more than ten years wouldn't show up. We could only cross our fingers and hope the truck's registration had been current at the time of the incident.

I began by entering basic parameters: the date at the time of the incident, the county, and so on. This returned a mind-boggling number. There were approximately four hundred thousand vehicles registered in the county at that time. Not to be deterred, I whittled that number down by removing trailers and recreational vehicles. I sorted for Ford vehicles, then I re-sorted, narrowing the search to a handful of zip codes.

I let out a sigh. I was still looking at more than ten thousand vehicles. And I wasn't able to separate trucks from all the other Fords. I explained the problem to Joe.

"Try weight ratings," he said. "This was a passenger truck. You can eliminate heavy-duty and commercial vehicles. Stick to half-ton and three-quarter-ton trucks."

That worked. I was down to just seven hundred trucks. "Still too many," I complained.

Joe peeked over my shoulder. "Are all those blue?"

I groaned. I'd forgotten the most important detail. Joe chuckled as I re-sorted the list. The number suddenly came down to forty. "There you go," he said. "Remember, *details are important.*"

"Touché." I shot him a glare and then turned my attention back to the computer screen. "Forty is still a lot. I suggest we start our background checks with those. If it doesn't work out, we can expand the parameters."

"Great, let's do it."

I started calling out names while Joe ran background checks on another computer. "Seventy-nine Ford F100 Flareside," I said. "Willard Kreese. 27 River Lane. Seventy-two Ford F150, Christopher Schatler, 417 Oak Place..." And so on. We paused now and then as Joe asked for more details on some of the individuals. It was important to be sure we were looking at the right person when comparing the two databases. I also kept track of the names, addresses, and matching vehicle models on a notepad. Next to this, I made a brief list of the criminal court cases for each subject.

Soon, we were down to eleven suspects. All had criminal records, all owned old blue Ford trucks, and all lived within a short distance of the crime scene. "Is it just me," I said, "or do a surprising percentage of people around here have criminal records?"

"This is California," Joe reminded me. "You can't leave the house without committing a crime. Besides, most of these are minor, especially considering that half these people committed crimes that are *no longer* crimes."

"Weed," I said with a shake of my head.

"Yep. Ten years ago, a possession charge could mean hard time. Now, it's no different than having a pack of smokes."

I checked the time on the computer. "That just took forty-five minutes," I said. "Not bad."

"Sure," Joe cocked an eyebrow. "You know most people get paid *extra* to work on Sunday?"

"Yes, but we have freedom."

We both laughed at that. The noise woke Autumn, and she began to cry.

Chapter 6

JOE

It was late afternoon when we got home. After a quick look through the pantry, Tanja announced that she was going to make her famous lasagna for dinner. That left me with a couple hours to kill, so I headed out to the garage to do some cleaning. I like to keep a neat, tidy work area. Instead, I tend to make a huge mess while working on a project and leave it that way for days -often until the entire project is complete.

There is a sound reasoning to my method: Why clean up and put away tools I'll just have to pull right back out? Better to get the job done, then worry about cleanup, right? Unfortunately, that means when a project is over there's a lot of organizing to do.

I spent almost an hour doing just that. I wiped my hand tools down with a grease rag and put them neatly back into their assigned drawers. I drained the oil pan from the Suburban's last oil change into a five-gallon bucket for delivery to the recycler. I even swept the floor and took out the garbage.

Finally, I was satisfied. And thirsty. I pulled a frosty bottle of beer out of the garage fridge and took a long swig. While standing there, I noticed my dusty old laptop sitting on the shelf above the workbench. I turned it on, thinking I'd find some music to listen to, or maybe something to watch. The moment I logged on, I got an email notification. It was a message from Sherry Breach, an old friend and local real estate agent. I opened it up:

"Joe, I'm contacting you regarding a conversation we had a couple of months ago. You said at the time that you were looking for a good property for your business. Are you still interested? If so, I think I may have found what you're looking for. It hasn't been listed yet, so please contact me ASAP. If I don't hear from you, this listing will go live very soon. Please check this link..."

I clicked the link, and it took me to a private listing on Sherry's agency website. The property she had in mind was a small two-room cottage on a good-sized lot at the north end of town. It sat on a busy section of Old Redwood Highway, just west of the town green.

I pulled up a stool to the workbench as I looked over the description. The property needed some work. The building had been sitting empty for three years. It had storm damage to the roof and siding. Also, because of a recent rezoning, it was now considered a commercial property and couldn't legally be used as a residence. That left the option of converting the structure into an office after rehabilitation, or tearing the whole thing down and starting over. Because of that, the owner was asking for a price that was a fraction of what it was worth. Basically, she just wanted the value of the lot.

I did some calculations and realized that with a down payment of around twenty thousand dollars, we might actually be able to get into the property. *But should we?*

Tanja and I had discussed opening an office on numerous occasions. The advantages were obvious: The increased visibility would lead to more business. Those profits would allow us to advertise and grow even further. The higher income and tax deductions meant the place would pay for itself. We could even incorporate, and that would financially protect us from certain business risks. But it was still a gamble. What if business didn't pick up *enough?* What if we got in over our heads?

In the past, those questions had always been enough to dissuade us. Well, those and the exorbitant price of real estate in Sequoia. After all, we had fought tooth and nail just to keep our home through the last recession. It had soured both of us on the idea of taking any more risks on real estate. Plus, after all that we weren't about to risk losing our home due to a bad business decision.

On the other hand, this place was *different.* Why? Because of the price, for one thing. It was the most affordable piece of property I'd seen in the Vine Hill area in years. Values had been climbing recently, which made it a reasonably sound investment. I was sure that if I had to, with just a little work I could flip the property and make a tidy profit on it. But that still left one problem. *Where was I going to get twenty grand for the down payment?* I leaned back, staring at the ad as I took another swig of my ice-cold brew.

Some time later, Tanja stuck her head out and said, "What are you doing?"

I glanced at the screen. "Uh, nothing... Just looking at porn."

"Very funny. Shut that thing off, it's time for dinner. And no, you can't buy a hot rod."

I smiled as the door closed. I turned back to the computer, proofreading the ad I had just created. My smile vanished. I held my breath and hit the *submit* button. Ten seconds later, I was looking at a live for-sale ad containing a dozen images of the *Agatha,* my lovingly restored sailboat.

I had spent the better part of a year working on that vessel. I had stripped, repaired, and sealed the hull with my own bare hands. I'd repaired and renovated the interior with new cabinetry and a custom bed. I'd destroyed God-only-knew how many shirts in the process of stripping, sanding, sealing and painting. Well, God and Tanja. I have a sneaking suspicion she keeps track of them.

I had even wired the boat for a small solar panel, so that it was perfectly useable as a live-aboard. The boat had a TV, a stereo, and working radar. It was an excellent, one-of-a-kind vessel, and worth considerably more than the asking price. And soon, it wouldn't be mine anymore...

It'll be worth it, I told myself as I shut the computer down. *At least we'll save fifty bucks a month in storage fees.*

Chapter 7

TANJA

We resumed our investigation bright and early Monday morning. After a quick trip to Robin's Nest Daycare Center to drop Autumn off, we were on our way. It was a cool, mostly sunny morning with patchy fog along the coast and near the river. The forecast promised another beautiful autumn day with an expected high temperature of seventy-four degrees.

I had a good feeling as we headed out of town. I was feeling optimistic, even looking forward to solving the case. I couldn't wait to see the look on Diekmann's face when I informed him that we'd solved a ten-year-old case for him. Plus, I really wanted everyone to know that I wasn't crazy -that what I'd seen the other night was real, even if it meant our search had been the result of some sort of unexplainable phenomenon. Better that than crazy.

"Next right," I warned Joe as we climbed out of a ravine near the south end of East River Road. "At the stop sign."

We turned onto a dirt road bordered by pastures of grazing cattle. A line of sequoias rose on our right, and eventually closed in at the edge of the field. There, we came to an old Victorian house with peeling paint and broken shutters. I commented on the sad state of the old building. It looked like it had once been quite beautiful.

"I'm more concerned about that," Joe said. He pointed at an old blue truck parked under the trees, away from the building. It was dinged up and rusty, half-covered in tree branches and needles. The windshield was cracked right down the middle.

I studied the windows in the house. No sign of life. "Let's split up," I said. "I'll go to the door; you go look the truck over. That way, they won't get a chance to say '*no*.'"

"Am I looking for anything in particular?"

"Body damage, of course," I said. "Check the bed, too. Jan said the driver had something in the back. See if there are any clues."

"Like what? Bloodstains from ten years ago?"

"Just look," I said. I headed for the house, purposefully trying to draw the attention of anyone who might be watching through those dark windows. Joe gave me time to get to the front porch, and then went scurrying off in the direction of the truck.

I knocked, waited, and knocked again. At last, the door opened. An elderly woman appeared before me. She had curly gray-blue hair and wore a loose-fitting navy-blue cardigan. In the background, the TV was blaring out a daytime talk show. Numerous cats were lounging on the living room furniture. The woman gave me a friendly smile and asked who I was.

"I'm sorry to bother you," I said. "My name is Tanja Shepherd. I'm an investigator working with the sheriff's department."

"Oh dear," she said. "Did something happen?"

"Not exactly. Is it all right if I ask you a few questions, Mrs-?"

"Kreese," she said. She reached out to shake my hand. "Marilyn."

"It's nice to meet you, Marilyn. I'd like to ask you about the truck in your yard. Does that vehicle belong to you?" She frowned, giving me a look that said she had no idea what I was talking about.

"The old Ford truck," I elaborated. "The blue one."

"Oh, yes!" her eyes lit up. "That's Willard's old truck."

"Willard?"

"My husband," she said. "He died six years ago. He had a long battle with cancer."

"Oh, I'm sorry to hear that. Do you remember if you or Willard ever had an accident with that truck?"

"Oh, I wouldn't think so," she said. "I haven't driven anything in years, and Willard -well he's dead, so he hasn't been driving, either." She chuckled at her own sense of humor. "Plus, it doesn't run anymore."

"I understand," I said. "I'm talking about something that happened a while back. About ten years ago."

Marilyn gave me a sideways look. "What did you say this was about?"

I paused to sort out my thoughts. The nice, helpful old lady suddenly seemed oddly suspicious of me, and on the verge of clamming up. "There's nothing to worry about," I assured her. "I'm not accusing you of anything. It's just that there was an accident down the road from here, and a witness saw a truck matching this description-"

"It wasn't ours," she blurted out, cutting me off.

I frowned. "How can you be sure? I haven't even told you what sort of accident it was."

"Because that truck hasn't run since ninety-two. The engine blew up. I kept telling Willard to get rid of that thing, but he insisted he was gonna fix it. He never lifted a wrench to it. He kept paying the insurance and registration on that junk heap right up until he died, though. Been sittin' there for decades."

"I see... Do you mind if I take a look at it?"

"Help yourself," Marilyn said. "In fact, help yourself to it, if you want. I ain't got no use for it!" She disappeared into the house, the sound of her hoarse cackling laughter fading as she disappeared inside.

As I walked down the porch steps, I saw that Joe was already back in the Suburban. "Well?" I asked as I climbed into the passenger seat.

"No bloodstains in the truck bed," he said with a smirk. "In fact, there's no bed."

"What?"

"It had a wooden floor. Looks like it rotted out a century ago. You can see the ground."

"Oh... What about the front?"

"No damage, except holes rusted through the sheet metal and the rat nests inside the fenders."

I sighed. "Well, I guess she was telling the truth. Let's move on."

He gave me a funny look. "Just out of curiosity, what did you find on this owner's criminal records search?"

I glanced at my notes. "Bankruptcy," I said with a sigh. "And a couple of judgments -probably for unpaid liens."

"Uh-huh. Sounds about right."

It dawned on me for the first time how hard this was going to be. All those vehicles... What were the odds they were still around? If the description was correct, that truck had been an antique ten years ago. Why would somebody still be driving it today? And what about the owners? Willard Kreese was dead. Others might be, too. Or moved away to a different state, or maybe even a different country. It seemed like long odds that we'd even find the truck if we searched every record in the county. It was like chasing a ghost. *Another ghost.*

I felt guilty for pushing Joe into this case. Maybe it was better to give up now. We had just wasted a few hours and a tank or so of gas. Was it better to quit while we were ahead?

I thought back to Friday night. I wondered if I had truly seen what I thought I had. Had my mind been playing tricks on me? Could it have been exhaustion, like Nate had suggested? It had just *seemed* so real. And how could I imagine something like that, just to have it show up in a cold case from an event that had occurred ten years ago? It was a little spooky.

"Well?" Joe said, pulling me out of my thoughts. "Which way?" I looked around. We had driven all the way back to the main road, and I hadn't even realized it. I wondered how long Joe had been sitting there waiting for further instructions. I glanced at my notes. The next two addresses were farther out, and in opposite directions. I chose one at random:

"Hillsburg," I said. "Fitch Mountain."

It was a fifteen-minute drive from where we were, but the challenge of navigating Fitch Mountain Road in a full-size SUV nearly doubled that time. The single winding lane snakes around the roots of an old volcano, climbing, twisting, and dropping without warning. The road is paved in places, but it's raw mud and stone in others. It's impossible to maintain -at least with any degree of success- due to the annual mudslides and constant traffic. The remnants of the most recent slide had been cleared out over summer, but the tarps and boulders still placed along the hillside above the road did nothing to boost my confidence.

"I hate this road," I grumbled.

"You say that every time we come here."

"How do people live like this?"

"You say that, too."

Eventually, we located a house built on stilts off the side of the road, stretching out over the hill above the river. The parking area next to the home was a concrete pad jutting out of the hillside, also supported at one end by stilts. A protective redwood canopy sheltered two vehicles in the parking space: A late-model white Mustang and an old blue Ford truck. It didn't look that old, though. At least not to my eyes.

"That can't be it," I said, noting the truck's gleaming paint and polished chrome. "It looks brand new."

"Better than new," Joe said. "That truck has been restored from the ground up. It has a six-inch lift and thirty-five-inch tires. The roll bar and off-road lights are all mods, too."

"You don't think this could be the truck we're looking for?"

"Depends on when the work was done. We'd better talk with the owner."

We eased onto the shoulder of the road and parked with half of the Suburban hanging out into the lane. There was -theoretically, at least- just enough room for another vehicle to squeeze by. The legality of parking like that was dubious, but it was common practice on the mountain. There were vehicles parked like that all up and down the hillside.

After a few knocks, a woman in her fifties answered the door. I told her who we were, and she introduced herself as Lissa Macguire. When I asked about the truck, she said, "Oh, that belongs to my son Derek. He bought it when he was in high school. Did a lot of work on it, too. He loves that truck."

"I can see that," Joe said. "Is Derek here?"

"Oh, no. He joined the army."

"When was that?" I asked.

"eight years ago. They made him a mechanic. He fixes everything, trucks, tanks, even generators. He likes it I guess, because he's still there."

"I see. Do you happen to remember *when* exactly Derek did all the work to this truck?"

"Oh, it was in high school. The school has an auto body shop, and that's where he learned to do all that stuff."

"So, about ten years ago, all of this work had already been done?"

She confirmed that it was. "Derek comes back a few times a year to take it for a drive and wash it," she said. "I keep threatening to sell it, but he knows I won't."

I thanked Lissa for her help, and for her son's service. She beamed with pride and said she'd pass it on. Back in the car, I couldn't hide my disappointment. "That's two strikes," I said. "Maybe I really am chasing a ghost."

Joe gave me a reassuring smile. "If we strike out, we broaden our search. We can keep looking at trucks all month if we have to."

"I know," I said. "But we really can't, can we? We have bills to pay. We have to get back to real life soon."

"True, but we have *right now*. Let's keep at it and see what we find."

Joe's enthusiasm wasn't for the case. It was a display of support for me, and that was touching. Still, I couldn't help feeling we were chasing something ethereal, something that might not even be real.

Four hours later, I was sure of it. And Joe's supportiveness was beginning to wane. We had been driving all day. We'd seen thirteen trucks. Well, a few of them had gone to the wreckers or had been sold. Of those that remained, not one had body damage in the right place, and all the owners had alibis. Of course, some of them might deserve a second look, but no one had struck me as dishonest. In fact, most of the owners had been surprisingly forthcoming.

I had always known physical evidence would be a problem. There wouldn't be DNA -not after so many years- but the dent might be there. If it had been repaired, then there should be evidence of that, too. And through the use of social engineering, I was sure I could manipulate a hit-and-run driver into admitting his crime. After all, the killer couldn't be a very strong-willed person. Not if he committed a crime like that. To accidentally murder someone and then hide the body is an act of high cowardice, and not a sign of high intelligence, either.

But I had forgotten one important fact: I'd never get a chance to coax the truth out of the killer if I couldn't find him.

"Last one," Joe said as we turned down a narrow dirt lane. The address was tucked in between the rural vineyards and mini-farms west of Sebastopol. The property wasn't visible from the road, and was only accessible by means of a narrow muddy lane that ran along the fence lines of two adjacent properties. I checked my notes.

"We're looking for Buck Tannin," I said. "He has a long record. A couple of drunk and disorderly arrests, plus an assault conviction. Buck did six months in the county jail for that. He's been arrested for drunk driving twice in the last ten years. He's also a registered sex offender."

"What *kind* of sex offender?" Joe said.

"I'm not sure. My notes aren't very extensive. I just wrote down the first few things I saw. I didn't look into the actual court files."

It was late afternoon, and the waning light cast long shadows around us as we drove down the road. A sense of gloomy isolation seemed to hang over the place, and that mood deepened as we approached.

The house was a two-story monstrosity, probably three thousand square feet, faded yellow and lacking any aesthetic appeal whatsoever. The closest thing it had to an architectural feature was a second-floor balcony made of age-blackened redwood that you couldn't have paid me to stand on.

The rest of the property wasn't much to look at, either. Passing through the gate, the soft blue glow of twilight illuminated the shadowy carcasses of half a dozen old cars sitting on blocks in various states of disrepair. Broken windows, peeling paint, and vinyl tops stripped into ribbons seemed to be the fashion. Tarps covered other vehicles, leaving just flat tires and rusty rocker panels visible. I saw piles of tires stacked under a nearby stand of Eucalyptus trees, and two old truck campers sitting on the ground nearby.

"There it is," Joe said, nodding. I followed his gaze to the object of our search. It was sitting in the dark shadow of that enormous house. I couldn't even be sure it was blue. It was the right make though, and the right age. The truck was old, rusted, and looked like someone had beaten it with an axe handle.

Joe turned the wheel, moving the Suburban a few inches forward. This movement brought the truck into our headlight beams. It was in fact, dark blue. And that wasn't all. "Joe, do you see that?"

He grunted.

Both of us were staring at the dent in the front passenger side fender. It wasn't a small dent. The edge of the bumper was pushed in, and the mangled sheet metal was twisted around the headlight. The yellow plastic cover on the turn signal light was broken and held in place by duct tape.

I caught a glimpse of movement in the corner of my eye, and turned to see a man coming out of the house. "Joe," I said, nudging him. He snapped out of it and followed my gaze to see the man walking our way.

The guy was big -husky, I mean, but short. About five-four. He wore an ill-fighting grease-stained tank top that stretched tight around his swollen gut. His shaggy hair was dark in color *-Maybe brown,* I thought, though it was hard to be sure in the fading light. Blurry, faded tattoos covered his bulky biceps. A big, black, mangy-looking shepherd followed him down the porch and across the driveway, its lips curled in a permanent snarl. Joe rolled down the window.

"You lost?" the man said, bending low enough to look past Joe and see me in the passenger seat. I caught an overpowering whiff of beer. About two cases worth, I guessed.

"Guess I took a wrong turn," Joe said with a grin.

The man glared at him. "What you looking for?"

"I'm not sure... What was that address, Tanja?"

I glanced at the sheet of paper and recited the address back, jumbling up the numbers intentionally. The man glared at us, but didn't say a word. Joe spoke up: "That's a sweet old truck over there. Is that yours?"

The man threw a glance at the vehicle, and his frowned deepened. "That truck?" he said, slurring his words a little. "That's a piece of crap." He narrowed his eyes. "Who'd you say you were?"

"Are you Buck Tannin?"

Any semblance of friendliness -or at least tolerance- vanished like a puff of cigarette smoke in the wind. After a long moment of silence, he asked in a low gravelly voice who we were.

"We're from Autumn's Hope Detective Agency," I said. "We're working with the Sheriff's Department. Is that your truck?"

Buck took a step back and his body went rigid. His hands folded into fists. Joe tensed up, and my chest went tight. Buck looked like he was about to take a swing at Joe. If he did, I knew how my husband would react. Worse yet, judging from his looks, Buck might very well be carrying a gun or knife. The situation could escalate quickly.

I had my 9mm tucked safely in my purse under the seat. I couldn't reach for it without attracting his attention. I didn't want to prompt the man into doing something stupid. If I had to, I'd step out of the car and grab it then. But if he did have a weapon, he might be firing already. Just one stab or shot at close range could be enough to kill my husband...

And what about the dog? I thought. If either one of us got out of the car, that dog would be on us in a flash.

My guts twisted up. A million things could have gone wrong in that moment. It was like watching a firecracker with a bad fuse. The fuse is lit, it burns, but there isn't any *boom.* All you can do is stare at it, wondering if it's a dud. You could reach for it, but if you do-

"You better git out of here," Buck said in a low growl.

Joe glared at him. Buck glared back. I touched my husband on the arm. "Let's go," I said in a quiet voice. The sound seemed to bring him back to the present, at least enough to remember I was there. With slow calculated movements, Joe put the car in reverse. We turned around and left. As we drove back down the lane, Buck was still standing there, watching us drive away.

Chapter 8

JOE

I knew Buck well.

I didn't know him personally, but knew his type. I knew what he liked, the kind of high it gave him, and how it affected his mood and thought processes. Crystal meth, marijuana, and beer. Lots of beer. That was the cocktail of mood-altering chemicals careening through this guy's bloodstream. The latter two I could clearly smell. The meth was obvious in his appearance and body language. More than anything, in his eyes. Tweakers are stereotyped as being scrawny, twitchy creatures. That's not always the case. Guys like Tannin are lazy, well-fed, and they can be surprisingly strong. They'll smoke, snort, or shoot whatever comes along. It's not about an individual high –it's a balancing act.

I suspected that Buck Tannin was involved in trafficking. He had the look and the personality -the environment surrounding him practically shouted it. He might have been cooking that meth in his nasty old house, but I doubted it. Buck didn't come across as that smart. Not smart enough to get away with it for long, at least. He was the type to either kill himself using his own product, or burn his house down due to his inattention to detail and his lack of self-control. He wasn't a cook; he was a user and very likely dealer.

Based on my past experiences with Buck's kind, I could just about guarantee that those beat-up old cars scattered around the property did in fact belong to him. He probably had a small safe or lockbox in the house that was full of pink slips signed over by guys who'd enjoyed the use of Buck's party supplies a few too many times without paying. After getting a couple grand in debt, he'd give them a choice: *Pay up, or sign over your car.* Being junkies, they'd take the path of least resistance and give him their wheels, which Buck would then contemplate fixing up, but would instead gradually tear down and part out for money. Cash, of course. Buck had to maintain appearances. He couldn't have money flowing into a bank account. If it looked like he had a real job, the disability checks would stop coming. I told Tanja as much.

I had a strong suspicion that somewhere on that property was an old Harley he'd been planning on fixing up. It was still in boxes -the same boxes he'd brought it home in, ten, fifteen, maybe twenty years ago. Buck might even have the know-how to put it all together, but he didn't have the self-discipline. Occasionally, he'd pull a few parts out of a box and grab a wrench and go to work. He'd get high of course, because you can't build a fat hogg without getting high, right? Then, after a few wrench turns and a few shots of WD-40 he'd do a little meth, just to get his blood pumping. But the speed would destroy his ability to sit still, and he'd have to smoke another joint to level it out. That would fix his concentration, but make him thirsty. So, he'd need a few beers...

I know all of this because I spent years working undercover in my twenties. Once, I infiltrated a SoCal motorcycle club and spent sixteen months working my way through the ranks. Nearly every person I knew back then looked and smelled just like Buck Tannin. They had bad skin and teeth, and wide eyes even when they hadn't slept in three days. And they all looked at least ten years older than they really were. Buck was in his thirties, but an uninformed stranger might have guessed he was closer to sixty.

The moment I saw Buck, I knew we had our man. Tanja knew it, too. There were just too many things about Buck that fell into place: the truck, the location, and the man himself. Tanja and I discussed this as we drove away from the house. We were in agreement on every detail. She hadn't been around guys like Buck the way I had, but she had studied them, and she could see what was plainly visible.

She was on the phone with Sheriff Diekmann by the time we reached the main road. She described our interaction with him and tried to convince the sheriff to bring Buck in for questioning immediately. Diekmann said it would have to wait until tomorrow. It was just as well. We were already late for picking up Autumn.

Tanja was up before dawn the next morning, which meant we were *all* up before dawn. By 7:30, we'd already had breakfast and dropped Autumn off at daycare. It wasn't until three hours later that Tanja got the call she'd been waiting for. We were at the house, working on paperwork when Diekmann called. I knew it was him from the way her face lit up when she glanced at her phone. Ten minutes later, we were downtown.

"You can watch," Nate said as he ushered us into the observation room. "The sheriff will do the questioning."

The deputy left us there. We sat quietly in the dark for ten minutes before Nate and another deputy brought Buck into the interrogation room on the other side of the one-way glass. Buck wasn't handcuffed. He had come in for questioning voluntarily. For the moment, there wasn't anything to arrest him on. Being a scumbag drug dealer unfortunately wasn't enough.

Buck sat in silence, glaring at the one-way glass. A minute later, Diekmann came in and settled onto the folding chair across from him. "I want to thank you for coming in today, Mr. Tannin," the sheriff said. "We appreciate your cooperation."

"I'm always happy to help our esteemed law enforcement officers," Buck said in a sly tone. I knew that mannerism so well I could have acted it out on a stage. The clever innuendo, the use of surprisingly sophisticated speech patterns and verbiage. These were all indicative of the career criminal's mindset. He knows words like *esteemed.* He knows how to use them, because he's absorbed it from countless hours of watching cop shows. But when asked for a definition, his confidence and articulation would fly out the window like an escaped parakeet. In other words, Buck knew how to appear smart, and possibly even *was* smarter than many of his drug-addled peers, but he was no professor.

"For the record, state your name and age please," said Diekmann.

Buck rolled his eyes as leaned forward on his elbows. "Tyler Tannin, age 36."

Tanja and I exchanged a look. *Who the heck was Tyler Tannin?*

"Mr. Tannin, do you own the blue Ford truck parked on your property?"

"Nah. That's my brother's. Why? Somethin' wrong with it?"

Diekmann threw a glance at us over his shoulder. "I see. And does your brother live with you?"

"You kiddin' me?" Tannin said. "You guys don't even know?"

"Know what, Mr. Tannin?"

"Buck's in prison. You should know that; You all sent him there."

"We did? When was that?"

"I dunno. Six years, I guess. Don't you guys keep records on this stuff?"

"Do you know what the charges were?"

Tyler straightened in his chair. "For real? Is this all you asked me here for? You lost track of my brother?" He smacked his hand on the table in disgust. "Don't you people know how to keep track of somebody even when you got him locked up in a cage?"

"I guess not," Diekmann scowled. "You're free to go, Mr. Tannin."

The sheriff's scowl remained as he opened the door to the observation room. "My office," he grumbled. "Let's go."

Down the hall, Tanja and I sank into his office chairs like two juvenile delinquents in the principal's office. Diekmann leaned back in his chair, folding his fingers behind his head as he glared at us. "I take it this is all news to you?"

"I had no idea," Tanja said. "I could have sworn he was Buck. He never actually said so, but he played along."

"We didn't get much chance to talk to him," I explained. "He ran us off too quickly."

Diekmann grunted. "Well, now we have a problem, don't we?"

"What's that?"

"First of all, that truck doesn't even belong to the guy I just hauled in for questioning. Second, you've alerted Tyler to our interest. If he's the middleman you think he is, Tyler's got all his buddies back at the house, cleaning up and getting rid of any evidence right this minute. Any potential we may have had for a case against him is gone now."

"Not necessarily," Tanja said.

Diekmann turned his scowl on her. She shifted uncomfortably. "It's just that Tyler thinks we're looking for his brother. He may think he just skated on a false alarm."

"That's true," I said. "He seems to think that we screwed up. I mean we did, but not in the way he thinks we did, if you get my meaning."

The sheriff looked at my wife. "Tanja, can you make sense out of your husband's gibberish?"

She grinned. "I'll try. Last night when we approached Tyler, we asked if he was Buck Tannin and if the truck belonged to him. And then he chased us off. That's it. He came here today and found himself answering questions about his brother again. From Tyler's perspective, we actually went there looking for Buck. That's all he knows; that we're interested in his brother."

"I hope you're right," Diekmann said, "because even if Tyler's not involved with this cold case, I'd still like to search his property. Unfortunately, I can't without cause. You two think you can help with that?"

"Of course!" Tanja said.

"Great. Let me know when you've got some good hard evidence, and I'll get a warrant. Pictures, preferably."

"Sure thing, sheriff."

Tanja was all smiles until we got back to the Suburban.

"What were you thinking?" I said as I backed out of the parking spot.

"What do you mean?"

"Why did you tell Diekmann we could get evidence against Tyler Tannin? We can't even get within a mile of that place now. If he sees us coming, he'll either shoot us, or have us arrested for trespassing."

Her smile vanished. She stared out at the landscape. "We'll just have to find something else," she said after a moment. "We'll find another way."

"Don't we have enough on our plates already?"

She looked at me. "I'm surprised you'd say that."

"Why?"

"I assumed you'd say the case is closed because Buck Tannin is already in prison. I mean, what's the point in going after him now?"

"Good point," I said. "I just didn't think *you* would give up so easily."

"I'm not. I just said that's what *you* would say."

I heaved a sigh. "Well, I didn't. I know you better than that. You won't rest until we prove what happened to the old man, or- Why are you grinning? Does that make you happy?"

"Sure does. It means I've got you trained."

I didn't bother explaining that she had it all backwards.

We decided our next step was to track down Buck Tannin and see if we could interview him. If he was still in prison, as his brother had said, we might be able to arrange a visit. But first, we had to pick up Autumn. There was no point in paying for daycare if we'd be working from home all afternoon.

On the way there, I made an unexpected stop. Tanja didn't realize something was up until I had navigated the roundabout at the edge of town. "Where are we going?" she said, looking up from her phone. "This isn't the way to the daycare center."

I didn't answer. We were just a few hundred feet away. I pulled into the parking lot a few seconds later and parked in front of the squat, single-story house at the west end of the large graveled lot. Eight-foot wooden fencing surrounded the property, giving it a closed-in, somewhat isolated feel. One old elm tree stood next to the building, casting a shadow on it. Other than that, the lot was empty.

Tanja gave me a confused look. "What are we doing here? Do you know someone who lives here?"

"Nobody lives here," I said, opening my car door. "It's for sale."

Tanja hurried to join me as I approached the old house. "Are you sure? There's no sign."

"I got a call from Sherry. It's not listed yet."

"Not listed?" Tanja stared at me. "Joe, why are we looking at this place? You know we can't afford to buy something right now."

"It would make a great office," I shot her a grin. "And it's a really good deal."

She crossed her arms over her chest. "It is?"

"Yeah. It's a fixer-upper."

"You mean it's a dump."

"It's not so bad. New shingles, some siding and paint... This place would be like new. I could even build a front porch."

She came closer. "Are you serious? Do you really think we could get into it?"

"Maybe. I'll have to talk to Sherry again, but the price is unbelievable."

She cocked an eyebrow. "How unbelievable?"

I winced. "Three fifty."

"Three hundred and fifty thousand? Joe, there's no way!"

"There must be," I said. "It's half the price of anything else in this town. And prices aren't going down."

"You're dreaming... Look, maybe you're right -maybe it really is a great deal- but there's just no way we can afford it. We could barely make the monthly installments, much less the big down payment. Even if we could get into it, we'd have to double our business just to stay afloat."

"But we could," I said, "if we had an actual office."

Her face softened a little. "It would be so nice, wouldn't it? Not taking business calls in the dining room, or having strangers show up at our house..."

She turned to look at the building, and sighed. For a minute, we both just stared at it. Then she turned away. "Forget it," she said. "Tell Sherry it was nice of her to think of us, but we just can't do it."

I didn't argue. "Maybe another deal will come along when the timing is better," I said. But I knew it wasn't true.

It won't, and you know it. This is the one chance you're going to get...

Chapter 9

TANJA

I spent the next day in the presence of dozens of rapists, murderers, and serial killers. Thankfully, the thick concrete walls of San Quentin State Prison separated them from me. The only one I saw in person was Buck Tannin -convicted six years earlier in the slaying of a gas station attendant in Santa Cruz, now serving a life sentence. That was the reason his status hadn't shown up in my background check. His crime, arrest, and sentencing had all taken place outside of Sequoia County.

"Nice tattoos," I said as Buck settled into the chair across from me. As the guard locked his handcuffs to the table, Buck glared at me with a look not unlike the one his brother had given me two days earlier. He was taller and better looking than his brother. A few years older, but had that same thuggish aura about him. The bad skin and teeth, the dark hair and faded tattoos -everything else about him was the same. *Two peas in a pod,* I thought. The Tannin family tree had a nasty case of rot.

Buck wore an orange prison jumpsuit. He had full sleeve tattoos that vanished under the orange fabric and reappeared above his collar to climb up the back of his neck. I saw dragons, mermaids, an Ace of Spades card, and some tribal artwork.

Some were professional; most were not. Those with color were beginning to fade, and they were all blurred around the edges. My compliment had been entirely facetious, and I think he knew that.

"You didn't ask for this visit to talk about my tattoos," he said. "Who are you?"

"Tanja Shepherd, consulting detective with the Sequoia Sheriff's Department."

He grinned, and a twinkle appeared in his sharp blue eyes. "Aha. What'd my brother do now?"

"I'm not here about your brother," I said. I showed him a printed photo of his truck. "Can you identify this vehicle?"

He shrugged. "It's mine. So what?"

Not a flinch or blink. Despite his pathological tendencies, Buck's body language was so far stereotypical. "Can you tell me how the fender got damaged?"

"I hit a tree," he said. He moved a little, shifting to the side. He kept his gaze fixed on me, but couldn't help blinking. He was being dishonest about something. I couldn't tell exactly what. Not yet.

"How long before you were arrested did the accident happen?"

Another nonchalant shrug. "Don't remember. Why?"

"I'm just asking out of curiosity," I said, "because this truck was used in a hit and run ten years ago, and I'm trying to find out who was driving it at the time. Obviously, it must have been you."

Buck's eyes widened ever so slightly, and his shoulders tensed. He immediately forced himself to relax, slumping back in the chair. The tell lasted for a fraction of second, but it was there. Buck knew what had happened, and I had been right.

"I don't know what you're talking about," he said. That defiant glare was back with a fury, and now his lies were even more obvious.

"That's all right," I said. "You don't have to confess. Soon, we'll have all the evidence we need. We know it's your truck, and when we find what we're looking for, you'll be facing another life sentence."

He made a clicking sound in his mouth. He gave a little shake of his head. He drew his gaze to the window and stared for a few seconds before coming back to me. I went on:

"Do you know what that means, Buck? It means you'll never get out of here. Until now, it was at least a possibility. Can you imagine what it would be like to be free again? To walk through the park, feel the sun on your skin? Play some football, or ride a motorcycle?"

A slight wincing look crossed his face. It was the motorcycle that got him. Must run in the family. I had him now.

"If you confess, you may get a reduced sentence," I said. "With good behavior, who knows what might happen?"

He leaned forward on his elbows. "I know what you're doin'," he said, "and it won't work."

"Oh? Why is that?"

"Because I couldn't have done what you said. Yeah, it's my truck, but I never hit anybody. And I can prove it."

"How?"

"I wasn't here. I was North Dakota, working the rigs. If you don't believe me, check my work history. You can even call my old boss. He'll tell ya. I worked the rigs for two and a half years, and never left town."

I wanted him to be lying, but he wasn't. Buck had such confidence in that statement that his entire being projected it. Sure, I would double-check later just to be sure, but I could tell that he had nothing to worry about. And I had no leverage. Buck wasn't the driver. It may not have even been his truck...

Except there was one possibility, an unlikely one, teasing at the back of my mind. "Who did you work for?"

"ACME Shale and Oil. My foreman was Graham Cillis. I'm sure he's still there if you want to call him."

"What location?"

"I worked in the Williston Basin the whole time. Lived in a tent for the first six months."

"Why not live out of your truck?"

He smiled and leaned back, giving me a calculating look. *Nice try,* his eyes said. I rose to my feet, smiling right back. There was just one reason not to answer my question. Buck was trying to cover for his brother. It wasn't working. I was now certain that Buck had *not* taken his truck with him to North Dakota. He'd left it here, with Tyler.

"I guess we're all done," I said. "Thanks for your help."

"No problem. You gonna put in a good word for me?"

I turned and left.

Outside, I turned my phone back on and realized I had missed a call from Joe. I was about to dial back, but my phone rang before I could. This time, it was the sheriff's department calling. "Hello?" I said.

"How'd it go?" It was Joe.

"Not great," I said. "I'll tell you about it later. Why are you calling me on the sheriff's line?"

"'Cause they took my cell phone," he said. "And you're my one call."

"One call? What does that mean? Joe, did you get arrested?"

He cleared his throat. "I'll tell you about it later."

Chapter 10

JOE

It was a foggy, gloomy Wednesday morning. The mist on the living room window painted a haze on the outside world. There was a dense humidity in the atmosphere and a smell in the air that foreshadowed rain in the near future. Next to me, Autumn stacked jumbo-sized Lego blocks into an awkward wall on the living room floor. The wall had a tower at one end, and the entire structure was tipping haphazardly to one side. When I reached out to steady it, Autumn pushed my hand away. She takes her castle-building very seriously.

It was just the two of us. Tanja had decided to make the drive to San Quentin on her own, leaving me home with our daughter. My wife possessed all the necessary skills to interrogate Buck Tannin; her expertise in body language and psychology were needed for the interview. My skills at -well, whatever it is I do- weren't needed. My presence would be more of a distraction than anything. And as always, it was a good idea to save money on daycare whenever possible.

Even though Tanja was right to leave me home, I have to admit being somewhat annoyed. The interrogation was an important part of the case. It could potentially be the turning point that would break the whole thing wide open.

Then again, it really was her case. Tanja was the one who'd stumbled into the old man's story. She was the one who had obsessed over it and dragged me along for the ride. So why not let her enjoy it?

Besides, it's important for a father to spend bonding time with his daughter. Even if that interaction is mostly the child telling him to back off and let her play, forcing him to realize that -at the ripe old age of three- she's already slipping away. Ah, the joys of parenting.

It was ten a.m. when I got a call about my online ad: *"Hi, is the sailboat still available? I'd love to take a look at it..."*

The buyer would be in Bodega around noon. He wanted to meet me there. I couldn't say '*No.*' Not with so much hanging on the sale of my boat.

Since Tanja had the Suburban, I borrowed Diekmann's truck. The sheriff knows we can't afford a second car right now, and since he doesn't use it most of the time, we have a standing invitation to borrow the old Dodge whenever needed. Diekmann keeps it at the sheriff's department, which is about a mile from our house. I loaded Autumn up in her stroller and headed out into the fog.

Half an hour later, Autumn was in daycare and I was on my way to Bodega Bay. For the entire forty-five-minute drive, I wrestled with my conscience. I hated the idea of dropping Autumn off like that. I hated missing out on that time we should have had together. And I didn't like doing it behind my wife's back, either. It felt like cheating -like I was keeping an important secret from my spouse. I mean, I *was,* but it's not like I was cheating. Strange how it felt that way, though.

On the bright side, I knew I had plenty of time to get to Bodega, show the boat, and get back home without my wife finding out. No harm, no foul. But who was I kidding? It was just a matter of time until Tanja found out. There's no keeping a secret from her. Maybe that's why it felt like I was cheating.

When I got there, it turned out that the prospective buyers were two men -a father and son team. The dad was a man in his fifties named Jaime. His son Carlos was twenty-five. They were looking for something they could use for extended trips up and down the coast. They had it all planned out: Mexico next summer, Alaska the following year. With a little experience under their belts, they might even brave a trip to Hawaii.

I showed them the work I had done to the boat, and explained how some of the electronics and accessories worked. I didn't have to do much selling. The boat pretty much sold itself. The men loved the *Agatha*, and since they had been shopping around for a few months, they knew exactly how good a deal it was. Quality wood-construction sailboats like the *Agatha* are hard to come by these days, especially in excellent condition like mine.

Half an hour after arriving in Bodega Bay, I was on my way back home with a big fat cashier's check in my pocket. And I no longer owned a sailboat.

I had mixed feelings about the whole thing. I had loved that boat. It had been a dream of mine to own a vessel like that for years. I'd put countless hours of work into it -time that I could have spent relaxing, hanging out with my wife, or taking my daughter to the park. Those hours were gone, and now I had nothing to show for them.

On the other hand, the money in my pocket was almost entirely sweat equity. I had invested a third of that amount into the boat, including the original purchase price. Not many people can say that about a boat. Plus, the money was going to something important. It was for our business; for my family's future. That's always the best bet, no matter what. While the loss of my boat closed off one branch of the future, it opened another, hopefully better one.

As I was driving, it started to drizzle. I had to slow way down. Diekmann's ratty old Dodge is not designed for speed, and definitely not for navigating the wet, winding roads between the coast and Vine Hill. During the long drive back to town, my thoughts turned to Tanja. I considered how I might break the news to her. I wondered how she'd take it. Would she be pleased with the decision I had made, or angry that I hadn't consulted her? I didn't see how it could be the latter, considering that the boat had never been her favorite thing. She had learned to accept it, maybe even taken a little joy from it, but I doubted the loss would break her heart.

And then my thoughts turned to the case. I wondered how Tanja's interview with Buck Tannin had gone. Wouldn't it be something if she'd coaxed a confession out of him? It didn't seem likely, though. Despite my wife's incredible talent for reading people, prying a confession out of a man who was already serving time might be impossible.

It occurred to me -not for the first time- that the Tannin brothers might be a dead end. So far, the only evidence we had against them was the truck. Yes, it matched the description, but that was it. We couldn't prove it had been at the scene of that hit and run ten years ago, much less who had been driving it at the time. Without a confession, what we had was nothing.

On top of that, my wife had promised to help Diekmann find evidence of Tyler Tannin's drug activities. I couldn't imagine how we were supposed to do that. It wasn't like he was just going to invite us into his house. If he'd never seen my face, I could have run an undercover sting on his operation, but now...

On second thought, staking out a drug dealer wasn't exactly rocket science. I'd done it many times. All I needed was a camera, a good stakeout spot, and a lot of time. Two of those I already possessed. I had several hours before I needed to pick Autumn up from daycare, and I had a very nice and somewhat expensive digital camera that Tanja and I used for business purposes -the very one that she had used to photograph that house up the coast.

Getting close to Tannin however, would prove a bit trickier.

That afternoon, I found myself cruising the rural roads surrounding Tyler Tannin's home. The place was locked in between mini-farms and vineyards, and was not visible from any nearby public land. I realized however, that one of the nearby vineyards was an L-shaped piece of property that butted up against the back of Tannin's lot. That, I decided, was my access.

A heavy mist was falling as I parked on the shoulder of the road. Overhead, the sky was dark. Rain was coming. I didn't mind. I prefer the cool weather of autumn to the summer heat. I just hoped it would hold off until I got some pictures.

I collected our five-hundred-dollar- digital camera from the seat next to me and slipped out of the truck. I threw a glance around to make sure no one was watching as I ducked under the overhanging grapevines and disappeared into the vineyard. The air was cool and dense with humidity, and the smell of burning firewood filled my nostrils. The leaves hanging from the outstretched vines were vivid with colors of crimson and gold, and they glistening with moisture from the fog. The branches splayed out overhead, reaching eight or even ten feet high. During the winter, they would all be pruned back to the trunks, but now it was like walking under a tunnel of interweaving fall foliage.

An inch of mud covered the hard-packed earth under the vines. I tried not to slip as I hurried through the rows, ducking from one side to the next as I made my way toward Tannin's property. The scent of fermentation grew strong in the air. It had been a week or two since harvest, and on the ground, discarded clusters of grapes had begun to rot.

Off to my right, I glimpsed the white picket fence marking the edge of a neighbor's property. As I skirted around it, a dog began to bark. I hurried past. Behind me, I heard the dog's owner yelling at it to shut up. The beast went quiet, and I heaved a sigh of relief.

When I reached the far edge of the vineyard, I hunkered down, camera in hand. There was a three-hundred-yard stretch of dead grass and not much else between me and Tyler Tannin's house. Patches of fog drifted by, obscuring my view of the property. The wrecked vehicles were dark shadows, and the decaying two-story house loomed over everything else forebodingly.

I heard voices, but couldn't see anything in the distance. I took the lens off the camera and activated the viewscreen. Zooming in, I caught a glimpse of Tyler standing next to one of the broken-down cars. He was dressed in overalls and wearing a pair of greasy leather gloves. Another man joined him, and they opened the hood of the car. I couldn't see their faces clearly, but I snapped a couple of shots anyway.

As I watched, Tyler and his friend produced a toolbox and started removing parts from the car. The combination of distance, haze, and shadows made it impossible to see exactly what they were working on. This process went on for about forty minutes before they disappeared around the side of the house and returned a few minutes later pushing a rusty old engine hoist. Now, I understood. Tyler must have sold the car's engine, either to the man helping him or someone else who would come to get it later.

I snapped a few more pictures as they pulled off the hood of the car and carried it to the side. The process of removing the engine took another twenty minutes or so, at the end of which the mist that had been falling became a drizzle. I was done. Tannin wasn't dealing drugs. Not today, anyway. And from the looks of things, he was done selling car parts, too. The two men were busy packing up their tools as I shut the camera off and carefully replaced the lens cover.

I turned to leave and came face to face with a big, mean-looking pit bull. The dog had a smooth brindle coat that might have been beautiful at any other time. Right now, the beast's exotic colorations only served to accentuate the snarl of its lips and its icy yellow glare.

The rain came down hard, splashing against my shaved head, drenching my jacket. I wiped the water from my face and gave the dog a friendly smile. "Hey there," I said in a low voice. "What's your name?"

A low rumble emanated out of the pit bull's chest. I threw a glance over my shoulder. Tyler and his friend were still packing up. They hadn't seen me. "Easy boy," I said in a soft voice. "Who do you belong to?"

"Satan," the dog growled back. Well, not exactly, but you get the picture. It was a snarl, and it evolved rapidly into a bark. And then another, louder bark.

I winced. I started backing away, trying to work my way around the dog and into the next row of vines so I could head for the truck. I threw a glance back at Tannin. This time, I found him staring back at me.

"Perfect," I said under my breath. I told the dog, "Go home," and pointed off into the vineyard. He gave me a demonic smile, proving just how many teeth he had. Left with no other choice, I broke into a sprint. The pit bull joined me. Now, the game was afoot.

I heard Tyler shouting from across the field as I sped through the vineyard. My boots slipped on the muddy ground, throwing clumps into the air behind me. Rain pounded down, blinding me, drenching my clothes. I reached out to steady myself, and heard the unmistakable sound of the hell-hound closing in behind me. I put on a burst of speed.

"Butch!" somebody shouted off to my left. "Butch, heel!" *Thank God.* It was the dog's owner.

I could see the road up ahead now. As the dog disappeared, I eased back to a safe speed. I came out of the vineyard at a fast jog, and turned left, in the direction where the truck had been. The moment I appeared, a spotlight hit my face. I heard the *crackle* of a PA speaker, and a voice said, "Turn around and put your hands on your head."

Chapter 11

TANJA

I hit traffic south of Petaluma. A few miles later, it came to a complete standstill. From then on it was bumper to bumper all the way through Santa Rosa. It was raining by then, and that didn't help matters. You'd think people who live in a place where it rains eight months out of the year would know how to drive on wet roads. You'd be wrong. Every time the sky clouds up around here, people go full stupid.

The trip back home took three hours; more than twice the normal time. I was a nervous wreck all the way, and not just because of traffic. Joe and I had just a minute to talk on the phone, and all I could gather from his call was something about a demon dog and then Diekmann getting furious and arresting him. Or something like that. Joe doesn't make much sense when he starts talking fast. I probably wasn't listening very well, either. Already, a creeping anxiety had begun gnawing at my gut. All I could think to ask was, "What did you do?" It was a question he seemed unable or unwilling to answer.

It wasn't just Joe I was worried about. Where the heck was Autumn? What had he done with my little girl? And what about our money problems? How were we going to pay for bail? Or a lawyer? We'd have to take out a third mortgage, and I didn't see any bank being crazy enough to fall for that.

Finally, around six p.m., traffic opened up. By then, I was just a few miles from Vine Hill. I stomped on the gas. Minutes later, I walked into the sheriff's department dripping wet from the rain.

"Tanja," Lucy greeted me cheerfully at the front desk. "Joe's in the back. Cell number two."

"Thanks," I said. I hurried down the hallway and went right past Diekmann's office. I opened the steel door at the end of the hall and stepped into the holding area. Of the ten cells, just two had occupants. A homeless drunk was in number nine, sleeping it off. I found my husband in number two, right where Lucy had said he'd be. Autumn was sitting on his lap, flipping through a storybook. They both looked up at me when I walked in. A wide grin split my little girl's face.

"Mommy!" she said.

Joe gave me a cheerful smile. "What took so long?"

I glared at him. A deep frown creased my features. "Joe, what is my daughter doing in a jail cell?"

"Nate picked her up for me. It seemed like the best-"

"Picked her up from *where?*" I demanded.

"Daycare."

"Why was she in daycare?"

Joe started to answer, but the door behind us opened and Diekmann came in. He glanced back and forth between us. Noting the tension in the room, he cleared his throat and said, "When you're done getting reacquainted, come to my office."

He handed me the cell key and disappeared. Joe approached the cell door, holding Autumn's hand. They stood waiting for me to let them out. I just stared at Joe through the bars.

"What are you doing?" he said.

"Thinking about how to get Autumn out of there without letting you out."

He laughed like I was joking. I wasn't.

"Marilyn Rothschild isn't pressing charges," Diekmann said after we had settled in his office a short while later. "You can be grateful for that."

Autumn sat on the floor next to us, pulling every single item out of her day bag. For the moment, I wasn't worried about the mess. She was entertained at least.

"Who's Marilyn Rothschild?" I asked.

"She owns the vineyard where your husband was creeping around."

"Ah, I see." We had been through all that. Joe had already told us his side of the story, and Diekmann had explained how Tannin's neighbors had called to complain about somebody trespassing. That was what led to one of Diekmann's deputies bringing Joe in.

"I wasn't creeping," Joe said defensively. "I was investigating. And I was doing just fine until that hellhound started yapping. Besides, I wouldn't have been there at all, if you hadn't asked us-"

This latter part was directed at Diekmann, who responded with a glare that almost melted the paint off the walls. "I asked you to investigate *Tannin's drug business*," He interrupted. "Not to go sneaking around his neighbors' properties."

"It's just a vineyard," Joe said, still defensive. "Besides, if it wasn't for that mutt-"

"Uh-huh," Diekmann said with a wave of his hand. "We've heard. Thing is, most people *like* the fact that their dog barks when strangers are around. Some folks keep them just for that purpose. A good detective should probably know that.

"Now, as I was saying, the *good* news is that Marilyn isn't pressing charges. The bad news is that Tyler Tannin has asked for a restraining order against the two of you, thanks to Joe's little adventure this afternoon." Diekmann turned his attention to me. "Tanja, I hope you learned something helpful from Tyler's brother, otherwise we may have reached a dead end."

My face was downcast. "I'm afraid not. Buck was out of state at the time of the accident. I suspect he may have left his truck here with Tyler, but I can't prove it."

"So, we're back to Tyler..." Diekmann spread his hands on the desk. "Well, in either case, I'm afraid we're out of luck. It looks like the Tannins are going to get away with it."

I wanted to argue, but there wasn't anything to say. Diekmann was right. Joe's arrest was enough to warrant a restraining order against us, which meant it would be impossible to continue our investigation. And it didn't look like Buck Tannin was going to be any help. Not unless we had something to barter. I couldn't imagine what we might offer, and I didn't picture a judge agreeing to reduce Buck's sentence. I didn't picture Buck incriminating himself either, or his brother. We were done.

We made the drive home in silence. It was a cold drizzly night, and the house was chilly and dark when we got there. A quick perusal of the fridge suggested our dinner would be either boiled hot dogs or frozen pizza. Neither sounded very appetizing, but we settled on the pizza since the oven would help warm the place up.

We had a message on the answering machine, so I pressed the button: "Hello," said a woman's voice. "My name is Virginia Wallurth, and I own a restaurant here in Cotati. I'm worried that my partner might be embezzling, and I'm looking for someone to investigate this matter. Please call me back as soon as possible..."

Joe groaned as I jotted down Virginia's number. "Another embezzlement case," he said. "Have you ever noticed our most interesting cases are the ones we *don't* get paid for?"

I didn't respond. I was busy calling Virginia back to set up a meeting. After wasting several days on a case that went nowhere, we were going to need every job we could get.

It was heartbreaking to fail on a case like that. I hated that Mary Martingale would never know what had happened to her husband. The couple would never find justice, and it was because I had failed them. Worse yet, I *knew* what had happened. I had seen it with my own two eyes. But since I couldn't prove it, my experience would now be remembered as the unfortunate result of an overworked mind, or perhaps an overactive imagination. The whole thing just made me want to cry, and I'm not the crying type.

Over the next two weeks, I tried and mostly managed to put the Tannin case out of my mind. Joe and I stayed busy. The mystery of Virginia's crooked partner took a few days to solve (he was indeed a crook) after which we helped a Santa Rosa couple locate their teenage runaway (he was still in town, living under the Third Street bridge with a dozen other homeless people).

After that, we took on security for a rock concert at a local winery. For that job, we had to hire a few temp employees. The logistics were a nightmare, but the pay was good -and at the same time we helped the owner figure out who'd been stealing cases of wine from his cellar. (It was one of his employees, of course.)

While all this work paid reasonably well -and in the case of the concert, you might even say it was lucrative- it was also rather tedious. As my husband previously noted, the day-to-day work of running a detective business is somewhat bland. It involves running background checks, doing paperwork, and endless hours of interviews and legwork. And taking lots of pictures. Lots and lots of pictures. In fact, it was this aspect of our work that led to an unexpected break in the Tannin case.

The break came on a Sunday afternoon, the day after the concert. I had just given Autumn a bath, and when I brought her into the living room to get dressed, I found Joe at the computer with our camera. We settled on the couch, and Autumn let out a whimper as I pulled a brush through her curly strawberry-blonde locks. I reassured her that I was going to be very careful. That bought me exactly one minute of cooperation.

"What are you working on?" I asked Joe as I pulled a shirt down over Autumn's head. Her hair wasn't done yet, but it was done enough.

"I'm downloading the shots we got at the winery. I promised to email them to the winery's lawyer... Oh, that's weird."

"What's weird?"

"Nothing... I just forgot these pictures were on here."

"Pictures of what?"

"Tyler Tannin," he said in a distasteful tone. "They're the pics I took the day I got arrested."

He had my sudden interest. I had been trying not to think about that case, but it had never left my thoughts entirely. I just couldn't forget that poor old man. "You took pictures?"

"Nothing helpful," Joe said. I put Autumn down and walked over to the desk. "I'd hoped to catch Tannin making a drug deal, but the weather turned. And then I got busted."

I smiled. "Yeah, I remember. You must be slipping in your old age."

"Ha-ha."

I hovered behind him, watching the images appear on the screen. I saw the blurred image of Tyler walking around his front yard with another man. I saw them working on the car, hooking up the engine hoist and lifting the entire engine out of the bay. While none of the images were particularly clear, it was obvious in most of them who Tyler was. But there was something else that caught my attention. Joe clicked on one of the images and sent it to the trash.

"Wait!" I said, grabbing his arm.

"What?"

"Can you undo that? Can you get that image back?"

"Sure, why? What's the big deal?"

"Just do it."

I leaned closer, looking at the shot of Tyler pushing that massive engine away from the car. "I think you did it, Joe."

"I did?" He leaned closer, trying to see what I was seeing. "There aren't any drugs... What are you looking at?"

I didn't have time to explain. I was already reaching for the phone to call Sheriff Diekmann.

Chapter 12

JOE

The sheriff didn't answer his phone, so Tanja left a message asking him to call us back ASAP. She then selected half a dozen pictures of Tyler and had me forward them to Diekmann's email. What it was all for, I couldn't even guess. I stared at those photos for another twenty minutes and still couldn't glean what my wife had seen in them.

Were drugs in the car somewhere, and I just wasn't seeing them? Was Tyler carrying a concealed firearm? Nope, couldn't see that either. *Just what had she found?*

Of course, Tanja wasn't talking. She often refuses to discuss the resolution to a case until she's sure it's right. Which meant for now, I could only wait. As luck would have it, something else came up to distract me. I got a text message from Sherry.

I forgot everything else as I read that message. The owner of the property we had looked at had accepted my offer. Earlier that week, I had taken a huge gamble -putting in an offer twenty thousand lower than the asking price. I reasoned that since it was an as-is sale, and in need of obvious repairs, I might have a chance. Turned out I was right. That was the good news.

Bad news was that my wife still didn't know, and I still hadn't figured out how to tell her.

In my defense, I hadn't expected it to happen so fast. I assumed that by low-balling the seller, I'd get an instant rejection. At that point, the real negotiations would begin. Instead, I was now committed to buying a property that I hadn't even discussed with my wife. Yes, I knew that she liked the idea, but she also said we couldn't afford it.

I went out to the garage. As far as Tanja knew, I was just cleaning and organizing my tools. The reality was that I was fighting an internal battle -one of the toughest of my life. While my offer wasn't necessarily legally binding, I couldn't pull it off the table now without risking the wrath of both the seller and my real estate agent. And possibly a lawsuit. But if I followed through, I risked the wrath of my wife and partner.

Yes, I'm well aware that this is how divorces happen. I was painfully aware of it as I read that text message over and over:

Great news, they've accepted your offer!

Six words. Six little words that were going to change my life. I picked up my phone and thumbed out a clumsy response:

That's great! I'll call tomorrow.

My wife appeared in the doorway with Autumn standing next to her in a diaper. "I'm thinking spaghetti," Tanja said. "Do we have any hamburger?"

I checked the freezer and confirmed that we did. Tanja went back inside. I smothered the urge to run down to the gas station and buy a pack of cigarettes. I hadn't smoked in ten years. I hadn't even wanted a smoke until that moment, and suddenly it seemed like a perfectly reasonable, rational thing to do. Instead, I turned on my old laptop and started browsing Craigslist, looking for cool old cars that I would never own.

Chapter 13

TANJA

I felt bad about keeping Joe in the dark, but I think he understood. There's nothing more embarrassing than thinking you have it all figured out, just to have it all crumble apart at the last moment. Better to get the footwork done first. Thankfully, we didn't have long to wait.

Diekmann made a few calls Monday morning. By that afternoon, we had Tyler Tannin in custody and were searching his home. No one was surprised when Diekmann went through the filing cabinet in the downstairs office and found bags and containers of various drugs. Tyler had crystal meth, heroin, and fentanyl in his possession. He also had ten thousand dollars' worth of marijuana in a big trunk. No longer illegal in the state of course, except for the fact that it was well over the one-ounce limit, and Tyler had no license to distribute. Not to mention the fact that he was not paying the required taxes. Altogether, it added up to a lot of years behind bars.

We were standing in Tyler's living room, surrounded by deputies. The place was filthy. It had a smell words can't even describe. There were holes in the drywall, stains and cigarette burns on the sofa, and the carpet looked like it was something installed in 1970 -and had never been cleaned.

"Well done," Diekmann said to me. "It looks like Tyler will be joining his brother in prison, thanks to you."

"Good," I said. "Let's hope they stay there a long, long time."

"I'll cut you guys a check tomorrow."

I thanked him, but I was obviously distracted. It was good to see Tyler Tannin get what was coming to him, but this wasn't the end I had been hoping for. What about poor Mr. Martingale? Where was justice for him?

I took a pair of gloves from the box and wandered down the hall to help search the other rooms. There wasn't much to find in the first two. They were Tyler's growing operation. The pot plants were tall, reaching all the way up to the high-wattage grow lights he'd mounted on the ceiling. I couldn't guess whether this was his lone source for the drug, but I doubted it. I had a feeling Tyler smoked his weed almost as fast as it grew.

The big room at the back of the house was Tannin's bedroom. It was dark in there because he had taped foil over the windows, and painted the walls a dark brown color. His bedroom was like a vampire's coffin. I had seen this before. It was to accommodate the crash at the end of a long binge. After being awake for three or four days straight, the user would crash and fall into a coma-like sleep. Clearly, this had been a regular practice for Tyler Tannin.

I started opening drawers. Joe appeared behind me while I was searching the dresser. "What are you looking for?" he said. "We've already got all the evidence we need."

"I know. I'm just looking for something else." I finished going through the drawers and moved on to the closet.

"What is it?" Joe said. "Just tell me and maybe I can help."

I slid open the closet door and caught my breath. There, on top of an old hardwood chest, was what I had been looking for: A jewelry box. It wasn't anything fancy; just a cedar box with a flip-top lid and several compartments inside. I flipped the lid back and sorted through the contents. I pulled out a small object in my gloved fingers, and held it up so Joe could see it.

"What is that?"

"A ring," I said with a triumphant grin. "A silver ring set with a red jasper stone."

Joe's eyes widened. "Is that Charles Martingale's ring?"

"Yep."

We both turned as Diekmann came into the room. He frowned as he saw me holding up the item. "What's going on?"

"I think you need to call in the cadaver dogs," I said. I explained where I believed the ring had come from; that I had seen Charles wearing it in the photographs in Diekmann's file. "If Tyler has this," I said, "there's a chance he hid the body somewhere on this property."

Diekmann went to make the call. I placed the ring in an evidence bag, and then we headed outside.

"So that's how you knew?" Joe said. "That's what you saw in the pictures I took? Tyler was wearing that ring?"

I frowned at him. "No, what gives you that idea?"

"I just thought... What was it, then?"

I giggled at his crestfallen look. "It was the engine."

Joe was baffled. "The one he pulled out of that Oldsmobile? What about it?"

"Remember when we first came to this place? Do you remember what you told me about guys like Tyler? You said, *'They're all on Disability. Scamming the system is like a national pastime for them.'*"

"Disability?"

"You were right. Tyler was accepting disability payments. Your pictures showed proof that he was defrauding the government. Nobody on disability should be able to tear down a car down like that. Your evidence allowed Diekmann to get a warrant. And now that we've searched his place, Tannin's getting charged with a whole lot more."

Joe could hardly believe it. "All this over a Disability claim? Who did I marry, Eliot Ness?"

"Nah, Ness got Capone on tax evasion, not welfare fraud."

"Close enough."

"Plus, I'm a tall, beautiful blonde."

"That's true," he said, pulling me close. "I'm a lucky man."

Joe gave me a long kiss, and then we stood there for a minute in one another's arms.

"So what are we going to do with the sheriff's check?" I said. "I say we take a little vacation. Maybe visit that castle in Napa."

Joe's smile vanished. "Yeah, maybe. We'll have to think about it."

"Is something wrong?"

"No. It sounds nice."

Joe's sudden distance concerned me. Whatever was bothering him, he wasn't ready to talk yet. I figured it would come out sooner or later. With Joe, it's best not to push too hard. He's got a lot going on in his head sometimes, and it's better to let him work things out. I knew that when he was ready, he'd share.

The next day, the sheriff called to update us on the search. It had taken all night to inventory and clear out the Tannin house. The dogs arrived at seven a.m., and within fifteen minutes they had located a body. The problem was getting to it. It was buried under one of the trailers, the floor of which had rotted out from sitting directly on the ground. In the end, they'd had to destroy the camper with the help of a backhoe. The same backhoe later uncovered the remains of an elderly male nearly six feet underground.

The victim hadn't been identified yet, but skeletal damage appeared consistent with the type of injury I had witnessed. Diekmann believed the remains were very likely those of Mr. Martingale. This was further evidenced by the presence of Martingale's personal belongings in the house. Believe it or not, Tyler Tannin had actually kept the poor man's wallet. It was in another box in his closet.

That afternoon, I went to visit Mary Martingale. I could sense Mary's reluctance to open the door after I knocked. I could hear her moving around inside -I even saw her peek through the living room curtains- but I still had to knock several times. She must have realized I wasn't going to leave, because she finally answered. She opened the door a crack, just enough to peek out at me.

"Yes?" she said in that thick Spanish accent.

"Mrs. Martingale, I have something for you." I pulled the ring out of my pocket and held it out for her to see. Her eyes went wide. She covered her mouth with her hands. The door swung open and she stood there, eyes brimming with tears.

"I believe this may have belonged to your husband," I said. "Can I come in?" She gave a nod and held the door wide. Tears were streaming down her face as we went inside.

Mary and I had a long conversation. She made coffee, and we sat in the kitchen and discussed all that had happened. Mary had long since given up hope of her husband ever returning. She assumed that something like this had happened. Deep down, Mary had known for years that her husband was dead. The legal proceedings that made it official were a mere formality by then.

She was grateful, but she was confused about how I had ended up looking into her husband's case. I confessed to Mary about the vision I had seen, and Mary began weeping again. She said she believed it had been a message from Charles. Now that we had found him, he could be properly buried and his spirit would be at peace. I wasn't sure how I felt about that part of it, but I was glad to see Mary get the closure she deserved.

Tyler Tannin confessed, but not right away. First, he threw his brother under the bus. When Diekmann told Tyler what we'd found, he tried to blame everything on Buck. Tyler said he didn't know anything about the old man, and had no idea how his body got there. It was Buck's truck, after all. Buck must have done it. The sheriff reminded him that Martingale's belongings had been in Tyler's closet.

"Our lab is checking everything for prints and DNA," the sheriff explained. "So if you've never touched any of those things, I guess you have nothing to worry about. On the other hand, if we do find physical evidence to connect you with the items in your closet... Well, that's about it for you. Or, if you want to confess now and save us all that work, I might have a word with the district attorney. We might even get your charges reduced from murder to manslaughter..."

Tyler Tannin confessed to everything. He'd been drinking that night. He hadn't even seen the old man until it was too late. Even after hitting Charles Martingale, Tyler hadn't been sure what he'd run into. When he discovered the body off the side of the road, he had panicked. He already had several DUIs under his belt, and was currently driving without a license. Rather than facing the consequences of his mistake, Tyler hid the body in his truck and then buried it on his property.

I wasn't too worried about the reduced charges. Tyler's confession meant an automatic sentence, and that was before the drug trafficking and possession charges, the fraud, and whatever else might pop up. Tyler was going to prison for a long time. If he ever walked out, it would be as an old man.

In the end, I don't know if it was Charles Martingale's ghost that started me on this quest or just my tired mind playing tricks on me. I realize now that it isn't the catalyst that's important, it's the result. Mr. Martingale and his widow finally have the justice they deserve. Mary has the closure of knowing what became of her husband, and Charles can rest in peace. As for me, there's still plenty of work to do...

Chapter 14

JOE

Two weeks after Tannin's arrest, escrow closed. Tanja still didn't know what I had done. Due to my substantial down payment and good relationship with the bank, they had fast-tracked the loan for me. That was good, because I was going back and forth about whether I had made the right decision. Plus, Tanja had been pressuring me to help her plan a vacation and I was running out of excuses to procrastinate.

The deal closed on Thursday afternoon. Sherry confirmed the closing via text message. Right away, I loaded the family into the Suburban under the pretense of going out for ice cream. On the way through town, I took a nonchalant turn in the wrong direction. A few seconds later, we pulled into the big gravel parking lot.

"What are we doing here again?" my wife said, looking up from her phone. "We already discussed this, Joe. We can't do it right now."

"I know. I just want to take another look."

"Whatever." She went back to staring at her phone.

I stepped out of the car, walked around to the other side, and opened her door. Tanja rolled her eyes at me. "What are you doing?"

"I want to show you something."

She heaved a sigh. My wife took off her seat belt and said, "Hurry. I don't want to leave Autumn in the car too long."

"No problem. She can come, too."

That earned me another eye roll and a second, even bigger sigh. I ignored my wife's testy attitude. I pulled Autumn out of the car and we walked up to the front of the building hand-in-hand. I stopped at the front door to wait for Tanja, who was a few steps behind us.

"Well, what is it?" she said impatiently as she arrived. "What do you want to show me?"

I pointed at the doormat. Tucked under the edge was a small white envelope. Tanja frowned as she bent over to retrieve it. She opened it up and found a key inside. Her gaze drifted back and forth between me and the key. "Joe... What is this?"

"Dunno. Why don't you try it?"

Tanja licked her lips. She stretched her arm out and almost reluctantly unlocked the door. As it swung open, she gave me a worried look. "Joe, what did you do?"

I beamed. "I bought a key."

Her chest rose and fell, almost hyperventilating. "Joe-"

"The key came with an attachment," I interrupted. "What do you think? I say we need a sign out front. And a front porch."

She looked faint. I put my arm around her and pulled her inside. There was no carpet, just bare plywood floors and water-stained drywall. "Don't worry," I assured her. "The damage is superficial. I can clean this up in no time."

Tanja stood there, soaking it in. She gave me a manic look that seemed to be hovering somewhere between laughter and tears. "How?" was all she could manage to say.

"I sold the boat."

"You did what?"

"The *Agatha*. I sold her a few weeks ago to get the down payment for this place."

"Why? Why would you do that?" Tanja punched me in the arm.

I wasn't sure what to say. I couldn't tell if her reaction was from shock, fear, or actual anger. "For us," I said. "For our family; our business. What are you upset about? You didn't even like that boat. You hated it."

She turned, pulled me in close. Tears were forming in her eyes. It's not like my wife to cry. She tried to blink them away, but that just made it worse. "I didn't hate it," she said defensively. She took a deep breath, blinking as the tears went streaming down her cheeks.

"Yes, you did."

A smile turned up the corners of her mouth. She couldn't help it. Soft laughter bubbled out, and she said, "Yes, I did. I'm sorry. I tried to like it."

"It's all right," I said. "You can make it up to me by cleaning up this dump."

She gestured as if she might punch me again, but broke out laughing instead. We were in a giddy, punch-drunk sort of mood, careening between wild laughter and heart palpitations. I don't know how long we stood in that room just looking at it, but eventually Autumn reached up to pull on her mother's sleeve. "Mommy," she said in a worried voice, gazing up at us with her big hazel eyes. "Ice cream?"

I laughed. "Oops. I almost forgot why we went out."

Tanja wiped the tears from her cheeks and shot me a grin. "Yes, baby," she said to Autumn. "We're going for ice cream now. Daddy's going to stay here. He has lots of work to do."

Saturday afternoon, Diekmann made a surprise visit to our house. He showed up towing a flatbed trailer and parked in the street out front. I couldn't see much of the tarp-covered car he was hauling, but I thought I recognized it as one of the wrecks from the Tannin property. I assumed he had stopped by on his way to the impound yard, hoping I could give him a hand. Tanja and Autumn were playing in the backyard, so I went out to greet him.

"Afternoon," Diekmann said as I walked up to the truck. He shut the engine off so we could converse.

"This one of Tannin's wrecks?" I said.

He gave me a nod.

"Need some help unloading it?"

"Maybe. Thought you might want to look at it first."

I gave him a confused look. "What for?"

Diekmann grinned. Instead of answering, he climbed out of the truck and walked around to join me. "Give me a hand with this tarp," he said. He started loosening one of the straps. I climbed up onto the flatbed to release the other side. A few seconds later, we rolled the tarp back to reveal the front half of the car.

It was my turn to be in shock. "Is this what I think it is?"

Diekmann grunted.

"This was Tannin's?"

"Sorta," the sheriff said with a shrug. "The previous owner signed off on the title and left it in the glove box. Probably a payment for drugs. That was fifteen years ago. Hasn't been registered since."

I shot him a perplexed look. "What does that mean? Are you saying *nobody* owns this car?"

Diekmann smiled. "In this situation, we usually just auction them off. We've already taken several to the impound lot."

I leaned up against the fender, staring in disbelief. The car was a 1937 Chevy coupe. Even in rough shape -rusty fenders, rotten seats, cracked windshield- it was still worth a hefty chunk of change.

"Well?" Diekmann said. "You want it or not?"

"Of course I want it!"

"Great. Let's get it in the driveway."

"Hang on," I said. "I have a better idea. I have a great place to work on this."

"Hop in, then. We'll drop it off. Then we can swing by the store so you can buy some steaks."

"You Sir, have a deal."

THE END

A note from the Author:

THANKS FOR READING *He said, She said: Ghost Story.* If you enjoyed this book, please take a moment to post a review, and don't forget to tell a friend!

Sign up for my newsletter[1] to access FREE STORIES not available anywhere else.

Visit my website[2] for info and updates!

1. https://www.subscribepage.com/JGatesNewsletter
2. http://www.jeramygates.com

Look for these exciting titles by Jeramy Gates:

He said, She said Detective Series
Valkyrie Smith Mystery/Thriller Series
Erased, a thriller
You may also enjoy the one of a kind fantasy/detective series,
Hank Mossberg, Private Ogre.
(Written as Jamie Sedgwick)

PRINT ISBN: 9798215149751

About the Author

Jeramy Gates is the author of numerous Amazon lists bestsellers in the categories of Mystery, Thriller, Science Fiction and Fantasy (as Jamie Sedgwick). Jeramy spent his childhood on a ranch in the Montana Rockies, but now lives among the grapevines and redwood groves of northern California with his wife and three children. When traveling, you may encounter Jeramy with his family and their three dingoes, camping in their fifth wheel trailer.

Read more at www.jeramygates.com.

Ingram Content Group UK Ltd.
Milton Keynes UK
UKHW010632220523
422140UK00001B/4